I have tried to recreate events, locales, and conversations to the best of my ability, but I was dead there for a little while. I've changed some names and details to protect the privacy of individuals and because I wish to make tenure.

Actually, maybe you should just think of this as a work of fiction. Names, characters, businesses, places, events, and incidents are either products of my imagination or used in a fictitious manner. If you think there is any resemblance to actual persons, living or dead, or real events, well, you're wrong.

Also, information in this book is meant to supplement, not replace, proper strength training techniques. Like any sport involving equipment, balance, and environmental factors, weight training poses some inherent risk. You aren't Barbarian Bill. Don't tempt the fates. Do not take risks beyond your level of experience, aptitude, training, and comfort level.

Advanced Praise for Operation Ragnarok

"Operation Ragnarok is a face-paced, irreverent nerdfest with laugh out loud dialogue, like Big Bang Theory on steroids. Suspend your disbelief and enjoy!"
- Dana Fredsti, author of the *Ashley Parker Plague Town* series.

"Hoist your geek flag with Operation Ragnarok, and remember to always bring your claymore with you when robbing a museum or trying to save the world!"
- Patrick Thomas, author of the *Murphy's Lore* series and the *Dear Cthulhu* advice columns and books.

"If you're a fan of Norse mythology, pop culture, action and humor this is the book for you! Operation Ragnarok is a wild romp of a read."
- V.L. Locey, romance author and mythology aficionado.

"A Dungeons and Dragons adventure comes alive with good friends and a hero who loves books!"
- Ann Myers, mystery author of *Bread of the Dead*.

"Let's face it; there's a little hell raising Norseman in all of us. So top off your drinking horn, shoulder your trusty Claymore, and board your very own Viking longship. Kevin J. Coolidge's "Operation Ragnarok" is about to set sail. Who says geeks and gamers can't save the world?"
- Max Hawthorne Author of the bestselling *Kronos Rising* series.

For Gamers, Geeks and Goofballs Everywhere

Operation Ragnarok

by Kevin Coolidge

We are all just killing time until time eventually kills us. Today I celebrated my forty-sixth birthday. Yippee, I'm one day closer to death. It's a little morbid, but it's true. No one gets out alive. Death awaits us all. What comes after? I've spent many a night thinking about just that.

Should I expect the white, fluffy clouds and the Pearly Gates of the endless jokes and cartoons? Is a pleasant Afterlife only available to those of the Judeo-Christian faith? Will there be virgins? Does it matter? Is sex even allowed in Heaven?

There are so many hang-ups about doing the deed on the Earthly plain that I can't imagine the situation improving once I shuffle off this mortal coil. What types of intercourse would be acceptable? Would it be missionary only? Is a hummer out of the question? What about breasts? Heaven doesn't sound so great if there aren't boobs. I'm not sure I'm interested if I never see a nice pair of sweater puppies again. What's the point?

People keep yakking about the definition of traditional marriage and whether it's a sin for two people of the same gender to tie the knot. I don't know, and I couldn't care less. I only know I'd end up getting screwed, lose half my stuff, and pay alimony, regardless of whom I married.

I was forced to attend Sunday school, and the only lesson I took away was that I should avoid apples and serpents, which brings up another point. How about meat?

My doctor told me to cut down on the amount of saturated fats, and eat more fruits and vegetables. Of course I'd have to eat more fruit and veggies if I cut down on meat! I'd have to fill the empty void of my stomach with something--like beer--since there wasn't enough protein and fat to fill it.

Is there beer in heaven? If Jesus could perform the miracle of water into wine, then there damn well better be an ice-cold beer waiting for me. Yup, if I can't get a nice T-bone steak done medium well with a greasy side of curly fries and a cold brew, then I'm not sure about the whole concept of "paradise."

I guess you could say I've thought about it a little bit. Who hasn't? When my friend Tom, the preacher, says our loved ones are in a better place, are they really? Everyone agrees, because we want it to be true. I want it to be true, but is it?

We go through life knowing death is waiting, but not knowing what comes after. We pretend that one day we'll march up to Saint Peter, stroll through those Pearly Gates, pick up a harp, and commence to be bored shitless for eternity. Our final reward awaits, whatever it is, but sometimes it's not as far in the future as you want. Death doesn't wait. Now I don't have to wonder anymore, because I died.

The sages say, a journey of a thousand miles begins with a single step. Mine started with just a single click. This is an epic tale full of danger, adventure, friends, a wolf the size of a bull moose, and fear--lots and lots of fear--and it all started on my living room couch.

My name is Kevin, and I'm an English teacher. I love teaching. I love molding young minds, inspiring hope, igniting imaginations, and fostering a love of learning. I love helping kids learn to think for themselves. Of course, it isn't always like that. In fact, it seldom is. I strive to generate passion. I often fail.

Teaching is frustrating as hell. I should be working on my novel, or reading, but after a long week of wrestling with bureaucrats, listening to poor excuses from students, and struggling to be politically correct, I'm exhausted.

I don't remember not being able to read. I've always loved it, and I love stories in all their forms. I enjoy a good movie. Cracking a cold beer and catching an old flick helps me to relax after my interaction with the public school system. I mean, I love my job, and treasure my students, but sometimes the bureaucracy causes me to forget that.

So, this story began as I was power-lounging on the couch my ex left after the divorce. She didn't want it. It's ugly, huge, and heavy. It's one of those sleeper sofas, and uncomfortable as hell, but I didn't have to move it again. I had just finished a scrumptious dinner of Salisbury steak, courtesy of Chef Hungry Man.

4

I was surfing the Internet and half-watching *The Vikings*, an adventure movie from the 1950's starring Tony Curtis and Ernest Borgnine. Those were the days. If you wanted something, you took it. The Viking Age was looking pretty sweet.

I've decided my youth was wasted. I wanted to be a pirate. What boy doesn't? Sadly, there weren't any classes on swashbuckling, or even sailing, in my rural town, and my parents wouldn't have paid for them anyway.

My father encouraged me to be something practical. Something that paid well, like an engineer, but I hated math classes. I did love classic science fiction, and wanted to go to Mars. My father suggested being an astronaut. I wanted to read.

I should have taken a stab at being a Viking, or taken more science classes. You can't go berserk in today's world--at least not without the consequences of probation or therapy, or both. Sailing the ocean blue, meeting exotic women, killing their husbands, or if things didn't go as planned, trading with the natives and drinking mead. It's a win-win scenario. My youth really was wasted.

With a deep sigh of regret, I scrolled through Facebook on my laptop, reading about how great everyone pretends life is. Meanwhile, Tony and Ernie were raping and pillaging their merry way across England on the TV. On my computer, I came across this interesting article about a museum that will sell you a real Viking longboat.

Reading on, I saw that the longboat in question was not a thousand year old relic, but a ship made with the authentic tools and methods of the Viking Age. That would be really cool. Who needs to nurse a mid-life crisis with a little, red corvette and a big-breasted blond if you can afford to own your very own Viking longboat complete with a fierce dragon head?

Now, if I only had the funds, or the credit, to purchase such a ship, I could raid the English coast in style. Who was I kidding? I'm paying alimony, and my Subaru wasn't paid off yet. Plus, I'd need new tires soon. The only thing being pillaged around here was my savings account, I thought.

My fat, lazy, orange cat jumped on the couch and curled up in my lap. I gave him a good scratch on the ears. "You know what, Loki? A respectable Viking wouldn't buy a ship from a bunch of stuffy intellectuals. A real Viking would steal this longboat. Scratch that, I mean pilfer it. Pilfering it sounds so much better than stealing, but I can't do it alone. I'm going to need a crew. I'll just share this article to my Facebook page so I can find it later."

Who would like to join my Viking crew and help pilfer this genuine Viking longboat?

"See, Loki, that ought to get me a like or two. I'll bet my left kidney that Tom responds before the end of the night. All this fantasizing is giving me a powerful thirst. Come on, cat, don't look so comfortable. It's time for a hearty drink of mead for me, and some tap water for you. I'll race you to the kitchen."

I decided it was time to stretch my hypothetical sea legs and get some exercise. I'd have to start training if I was going to be raiding the coast. It's only twenty feet from the living room to the kitchen, but it was a start. I promised myself that Monday, I'd start back in the gym with Bill.

I opened the refrigerator aaaaand... I guessed I'd be settling for a Pabst Blue Ribbon. I popped the beer and went back to the couch to finish my movie and check my messages. I saw my post on the Viking longboat already had thirteen likes, and everyone in my Dungeons & Dragons group had made a comment. Yup, Tom was the first.

Tom: I'll bring the beer.

Bill: HAVE YOU GUYS SIGNED MY ONLINE PETITION YET?

Annette: Make sure Bill wears at least a loincloth if he comes.

Barry: Are you able to go fishing in it?

James: Remember we start a new campaign tomorrow. Be nice to your DM and he'll be good to you.

I always say: If you are going to dream, shoot for the stars, that way if you fail, you'll be in the cold vacuum of space, and no one will hear you scream. I quaffed my beer, and shut down my laptop for the night.

I'm a lifelong gamer--board games, RPG games, video games. Ahh, video games, I remember when the arcade game *Gauntlet* was new. I always played the Warrior and James was always the Wizard. No surprise that Annette just had to be the Valkyrie. Her brother Tom would always choose the annoying Elf. Barry was too cheap to feed a machine a constant stream of quarters.

That was good news for us. He saved his money for food, books, and *Dungeons & Dragons*. Our gaming group is so old that we like to say we played *Dungeons & Dragons* before it became D&D, but it isn't true. *D&D* had been out for a few years when I rolled up my first character, but James had the rules to *The Fantasy Game* and *Chainmail*, which would eventually evolve into the most successful RPG in the world, the role-playing game we play almost every Friday night.

I was enamored from the very beginning. Talk of invisibility rings and healing potions in the school hallway, and being able to be a Hobbit, just like in my favorite book. Looking back, those first games were juvenile and silly, especially as my fighter liked to run around with a sword easily as big as he was. It was a blast.

Some things never change. We still get together once a week to play *D&D*. Sometimes a little more in the winter months, and over Christmas break; a little less during finals week, depending on everyone's schedule.

We're seasoned veterans, which is a polite way of saying we've earned our experience points the hard way, but on occasion we'll invite a newbie. Sometimes they play through an entire campaign, more often they get devoured by cave trolls.

We're old school. We use paper, pencil, graph paper, and lots and lots of dice. Sometimes the miniature actually matches our character, and once in a blood moon, Barry will break out his calculator instead of doing the math in his head. We prefer 2nd edition, mostly because among us we own all the manuals. We modify when we want and stick to the rules when it suits us. We play for fun.

James is our regular DM. He's pretty much our only DM. We've let Barry run a campaign or two. He's a great cleric. He's steady, stoic, dependable with a blessing, and deals out massive damage with his artifact mace, but he's lacking in imagination. To be blunt, Barry's a boring DM.

James looks like it's still 1987. His hair is still long. I don't think he owns a shirt that isn't black. He mostly wears band T-shirts, and has the pale complexion of a troglodyte. It's his natural coloring.

He's a redhead. He doesn't tan. He freckles or he burns--or he used to. He seldom goes outside anymore. I did say we were old school. We still do a lot of dungeon crawls.

It was the night after I posted about the Viking longship. James was looking paler than usual, even a little yellowed around the edges--like an old thrift store paperback. It was a stark contrast to the black cut-out castle he uses as a Dungeon Master screen. He looked over to where I was sitting at the kitchen table.

"So, you're in a tavern..." James began.

"Always with the tavern. Have you ever created a campaign that didn't start in a tavern?" I replied.

"Yes, remember that time when the party woke up in a kobold pit covered in excrement and with amnesia?" answered James.

"Tavern it is. My bard is sitting over at the corner table, drinking a large mead," I said.

"I don't remember the kobold pit," said Tom. Tom, our resident thief, snatched a twenty-sided die, tossed it back and forth between his hands and rolled a perfect, natural 20.

"It's time for my rap. It's not crap. I'm the party's thief, and it's a trap! Well, if there's a trap, I just found it. So, Mister DM, is there a trap?" Tom rapped.

Tom might play a thief, but he's our harlequin, our court jester, our fool. His character is quick with a back stab, and even quicker with a joke. He's got a great sense of humor. He claims it's essential for his profession, or he'd never make his saving throws. He's a priest.

James rolled his eyes in the way that only the most experienced DMs can do, and with an exasperated sigh said, "Yes, you find and disarm a poison needle in the stem of your wine glass. It's a public tavern. There aren't any

10

traps. At least not yet..." chuckled James.

"Is it time to fight yet?" asked Bill.

Bill is big, brawny, and blond. He's our barbarian fighter with a tendency to go berserk. He'd make an excellent Viking. He's our youngest player. He's only in his mid twenties--twenty five, I think. He attends college, or at least starts most semesters. He loves it so much he may never leave. He's on the decade plan.

Bill works part-time in a college bar for beer money and the view. He likes to call himself "The Cooler", because he's watched *Roadhouse* with Patrick Swayze almost as many times as he's watched *Highlander*. He seldom has to "bounce" anyone. He mostly checks IDs at the door, and watches the pretty girls jiggle on the dance floor.

Bill is a big guy though, and he doesn't usually have to ask the troublemakers twice to settle down. He's a gentle giant, and prefers to get his workouts in the gym, but I've seen him toss out linebackers like he was pitching hay bales.

James enjoys how Bill plays his character. We all do. He's gruff and wild and quick to jump into a fight, any fight, but he always has the party's back. He reminds me of my favorite *Conan* movie--the original, not the cheesy sequel with Wilt Chamberlain.

"No, it's time to be recruited for the adventure, and then you'll have the opportunity to get in a tavern brawl," explained James.

"I stab the Hobbit in the eye," quipped Tom as he rolled yet another natural 20.

"No, no, no, you can't call them Hobbits anymore! The Tolkien estate has a standing cease-and-desist against Gygax and TSR, or Wizards of the Coast, or whoever. It's a halfling! You know that!" yelled James.

"Hey, you aren't using one of those trick die again, are you? That's your second natural 20 tonight, and we haven't even gotten to the combat yet," asked James.

Tom brought his hands up to his chest and cupped his pectorals. "Why, yes they are real. How kind of you to notice," said Tom.

A big grin lit up Bill's face. He slammed down his two liter bottle of Mountain Dew and announced, "He's a natural."

Annette groaned and popped a bright orange cheese curl into her mouth, then wiped her hands on her pants. Annette is a tall, statuesque blond, and is our fighter. Oh, and she plays a half-elf archer in the game.

It wasn't common for the gentler sex to participate in role-playing games when I was growing up. You'd see advertisements in *Dungeon Magazine*, and there'd always be a cute girl in there, but that was the closest most gamers got to a female. Remember the *Dungeon & Dragons* cartoon from the 80s? It had two girls. Count 'em, two girls. We had Annette.

"You don't look well, James. Have you been up late reading *Beowulf* or the *Silmarillion* again?" asked Annette.

It was a trick question. James was always up late. He worked the graveyard shift at the local glass factory. He preferred the night shift, because he didn't have to deal with management, could sleep all day, and spend his bennies reading or developing our next adventure.

"Actually," replied James. "I'm currently delving into the Icelandic sagas. I'm researching my mother's side of the family, but I guess you could say my constitution hasn't exactly been an eighteen lately."

Barry finally spoke up, "Fail your saving roll?"

Barry is the oldest of our party. He's a big, burly guy with a beard, and he's strong as a half-ogre, even though his idea of being active is a fishing reel in one hand, and a beer in the other. His beer belly is starting to turn into a keg.

He's pretty quiet until you get to know him, and then he's pretty quiet. He's introverted and comes across as conservative, but he is a certified public accountant. So, maybe it's safe to say that he just doesn't take risks. He loves the fantasy genre, and his cleric is a great addition to the party--dependable, steady, good in a fight; that's Barry.

"Ha, you look a little like I did when I was taking all that beta carotene for a bodybuilding contest," said Bill.

"I remember that. You looked like a giant, fucking carrot," I laughed.

13

James idly rolled a couple of dice, and looked at Barry. "You could say that. I haven't had much of an appetite, or been sleeping that well. I've been working too much overtime, and not getting much natural sunlight. I figured I'd try some of those tanning pills. A little extra vitamins never hurt anyone. Maybe I should see a healer."

"Does that mean you aren't going to 'Finnish' your sub," quipped Bill.

Bill is such a big, goofy guy, that sometimes I forget the weird sense of humor that flows under his surface, and can he ever eat! Damn, I wish I could still eat like that and not have to worry about fitting into my dress shirts for school.

"How did you know? I haven't even taken it out of my bag of holding yet," said James.

"Dude, I can smell Subway from here," Bill replied.

I couldn't wait any longer to talk about the Viking longboat. I'd been thinking about it since I posted it. "Speaking of subs, I was reading an article on Facebook about..."

Bill was so excited that he didn't wait for me to finish, "Hey, that reminds me, have you guys signed my petition for *'Bring Your Claymore to Work Day'* yet? It's really important to me."

Everyone in the room rolled their eyes and said, "YES, BILL!"

Annette chimed in, "Bill, not everyone has seen *Highlander* a thousand times. As a matter of fact, not

14

everyone has a claymore, or even knows what a claymore is."

"I thought of that," replied Bill, "That's why I added *'Or Other Big Damn Sword'* I don't personally see why you'd want anything else, but I'm cool with longswords, or even your occasional falchion sword. Leave the polearms where they belong though...on the wall."

"Ah-hem!" I tried to bring the conversation back to the topic of the Viking longship. "As I was saying, I was reading about a museum that will sell you a genuine Viking longboat," I said.

"You mean a thousand year old boat? What are you going to do with that other than show it in a museum?" said Barry.

"No! A brand new boat that is built with the traditional methods of the period, with tools and techniques from the Viking Age," I replied.

"That'd be cool," said Bill.

"It's time-intensive, and expensive. I wish I had the funds available to purchase this piece of living history," I replied.

"Buy? You want to purchase this vessel? A Viking wouldn't buy the boat. Wouldn't a real Viking put together a raiding party, and steal the boat?" Tom said.

"That's what I thought, Tom!" I answered excitedly.

"Hmmm, I always wanted to be a pirate," said Annette.

"You can't be a pirate. You're a girl," said Bill.

Annette gave Bill a sharp jab in the shoulder. "I'm a marine. I'm already a damn pirate. Just add rum."

Telling Annette that she can't do something because she's a female works about as well as telling a barbarian that he has to have the lock-picking skill to open the door.

Annette joined the Marines after high school and is a veteran of Desert Storm. That's where she lost the leg. She never talked about it, and I never wanted to ask. Once though, Tom did tell me friendly fire--isn't.

She refused to let it slow her down. She used the GI Bill to go to college after she got out of rehab, and became a teacher. She said the Gulf War taught her where Kuwait was, and she should return the favor.

"I do have a lot of accumulated vacation time," Barry mused.

Barry always has a lot of vacation time. He hates vacation. He'll only take a week during July to go fishing with his brother-in-law. His wife nags him to take it. He hates fishing. I don't know why he even bothers.

"Well, we can't just waltz into a museum and steal an entire ship," I said.

"Of course not," said James. "That's why we need to plan it."

"I've seen every *Conan* movie," said Barry.

"I'll bring the beer," said Tom.

Barry isn't done speaking yet. "I've even seen the soulless remake with the Dothraki. I've even seen *Krull* and

16

Beastmaster, for Crom's sake."

I didn't see where watching sword-and-sorcery movies was preparation for stealing a Viking longboat, but Barry was usually a man of few words, and it appeared he was getting excited and wanted to contribute to the conversation.

I know Tom was exhilarated. I never had to guess with Tom. He was enthusiastic. "I finally have a good excuse to wear my Viking beer helmet!"

"Like you need an excuse," smirked Annette. "Furthermore, the Vikings did NOT wear horned helms, and there is no such thing as a Viking beer helmet!"

"There is, too," retorted Tom. "I bought it on Ebay when I bought my *Sting* letter opener."

"Sounds like we should have Tom roll for initiative," I said.

"I have the beard. I might as well be a Viking," said Barry. I hadn't heard Barry say this much since his wife suggested he take two week's vacation.

The excitement breathed a little more color to James's face. "It would be the adventure of a lifetime. I've always wanted to sail the 'whale-road'."

"If you are talking like a skald, I figure you must be feeling better," said Annette.

Tom broke out into his best Elmer Fudd impression. "I've been working on the 'whale-road' all the wive wong day."

"Whales?" questioned Bill. "I thought Viking ships had big, scary dragon heads with big, pointy teeth, and what's a skald?"

"'Whale-road' is a kenning for the ocean, and a skald is a poet or singer, basically a bard," lectured Annette.

"I'm pretty keen on the ocean. I'd love to learn to surf, but the college doesn't offer classes," said Bill.

"No, KENNING. It's a figurative expression of speech that replaces a name or noun. Often it is a compound of two words and the words are hyphenated. Kenning are usually associated with Old Norse or Icelandic poetry," continued Annette.

"Thanks, teach," said Tom.

"So, Kevin is basically our skald?" asked Bill.

"Actually, yes, that's basically correct. Although the word skald is generally used for poets who composed at the courts of Scandinavian and Icelandic leaders during the Viking Age and Middle Ages," said Annette.

"Well, I hate fishing. I am NOT going fishing this year, damn it!" exclaimed Barry.

"What is best in life?" shouted James.

The room was buzzing. Everyone was standing up. Bill was pumping his fist into the air. Barry's forehead was covered in sweat. The room echoed with, "To crush your enemies, to see them driven before you, and to hear the lamentations of the women!"

James looked more alive than I have ever seen him, "Let's steal the Viking longship!!!"

It was a great night of gaming. We brawled with the city guard, because the captain of the watch decided to proposition Annette's half-elf character. She could have forgiven that, but the pat on her ass--big mistake. Tom's thief was able to fast-talk the local magistrate into letting us go, on the condition we would ~~assassinate~~ I mean eliminate with extreme prejudice a chaotic evil magic user that was disturbing local trade routes. Turned out to be a lich.

We gamed long into the night. Screw the dawn; this was our time to shine, we creeped into the Lich's lair leaving only a lifeless corpse. Okay, so it was a lifeless corpse when we got there, but it was throwing fireballs and commanding un-dead legions. Flames danced in soulless eye sockets. We snuffed that lich's candle. No one in the party could have managed it on their own, but together we kicked its bony pelvis, good times.

It was cold, frosty, and late by the time we divided up the treasure, and Annette's character found a magic dagger to replace the one she had lost. I offered James a ride. He walks everywhere. If I'm driving up East Avenue at night, and see a red dot bobbing along, I know it's James.

"I really wish you'd give up those damn cigarettes," I said.

"Yeah, I know. It's nasty. Picked it up working at the factory. They calm my mind and give my hands something to do," said James.

"My old man always called then 'coffin nails'. They'll end up killing you," I said.

"My grandpa smoked cheap cigars and drank Jim Beam every day, and he lived into his eighties. Besides, something has to kill me, right? No man escapes his wyrd," said James.

"What's weird" I asked, not following him.

"What's weird is that Barry goes fishing every damn summer even though he hates it. We all see it, but I was talking about the Anglo-Saxon concept corresponding to personal destiny. It's like fate, and no one escapes their fate. I refuse to die before my time," said James.

"Well, you'd have more money in your checking account," I said.

"You don't smoke and you're broke," replied James.

"I tempted fate by marrying a harpy," I joked as I pulled into James's driveway. It wasn't a big house, but it was all his. One of the advantages of a steady paycheck and being a perpetual bachelor.

"You have a good night, James, what's left of it. I can't believe that we were able to defeat the lich. I thought we'd lost the thief forever after he failed his saving throw, but Barry brought him back. That was the most fun I've had in ages," I said.

"We'll have to see if you can do it next week now that the lich knows you're coming," said James slyly.

"That lich was toast. You'll have to come up with something better," I said smugly.

"The party spent all that time helping the half-elf look for a new dagger, but no one thought to search for the phylactery. It's where the lich keeps his soul," chuckled James as he rubbed his chin.

"Damn! How did I not think of that? Especially after reading Harry Potter!" I exclaimed.

"It's the things you never think of that end up killing you," said James. "I think I'm going to skip shaving this week. A Viking should have a good beard. I'll look good in a beard. Maybe you should start one?" said James.

"Me with a beard? Now that would be weird. I don't think we should tempt fate," I said.

I've always enjoyed reading, and share that love with Annette. We often pass books back and forth, so when she asked me to tag along to visit our town's only bookstore, I couldn't say no.

She wanted to bone up on her Norse Mythology. I wanted to grab a new read and check out the cute brunette that works there. Turned out Annette had the same idea.

When we walked through the door, a glass chime rang out our presence. The bookstore clerk looked up from shelving books. A big, sleek black cat was napping on the counter.

"Could you tell me where the folklore section is?" asked Annette.

"It's right over there next to the poetry," answered the clerk.

"Where's the survival section?" I asked.

"Well, we have the *Zombie Survival Guide* by Max Brooks. It's really funny, and when I saw Max speak at Mansfield University, he told the audience that people have actually used the book in a survival situation, not against zombies, of course, but, you know, like survival stuff," said the clerk.

"That's OK. We won't be running into any zombies where we are going," I said.

"He means like Navy Seal manuals, or martial arts, maybe a good knife-fighting book, or a book on Viking warfare," interrupted Annette.

"And a good book on knots," I added.

"Oh, you mean like Paladin Press? Yes, those are right next to the homesteading and gardening books, two rows over. I know we have a good book on fishing knots," said the clerk.

"Maybe we should get that for Barry," laughed Annette.

Annette wandered over to browse the folklore section. She selected two titles, *D'Aulaires Book of Norse Myths* and *Nordic Gods and Heroes,* and took them up to the cash register. The cat still hadn't moved.

"Oh, I just love Norse folklore. Someone must have seen *Thor*. I think Chris Hemsworth is sooooo dreamy. I can't wait to see him in *Thor: Ragnarok*," sighed the clerk.

"I did watch it, but found it a little too homo-erotic for my tastes, though not as extreme as Zach Synder's *300*. I mean, come on. You're going into mortal combat with the Persians and forget to pack armor, but remember your G-string," commented Annette.

"Unbearably buff men hanging out with other unbearably buff men, what's not to like? Yummy," said the clerk.

"Wasn't *300* originally a graphic novel?" I interrupted.

"It's by Frank Miller. We don't have it in, but we can order it for you," replied the clerk.

"The first *Thor* just barely squeaks past the Bechdel test, and with all those Valkyries hanging around Asgard, Thor has only one female friend? Where are the strong female role-models?" demanded Annette.

A look flowed across the clerk's face. If you've ever worked customer service, you know it can be difficult to know just when you should begin a conversation with a customer and when it's best to shut your mouth. With

Annette, it's usually best to just keep quiet. I could tell that the clerk was sorry for mentioning her appreciation of Thor's chiseled physique.

"Do you need a bag?" asked the clerk. She looked like she couldn't wait to get back to shelving books. The miniature black panther on the counter still hadn't moved.

"Thor's hammer is obviously a phallic symbol. It's fine to have a mighty hammer, or a penis, but you don't have to swing it around and show it to everyone. Yes, I would like a bag, please. It looks like a storm is brewing. Hope I didn't anger the god of thunder. I'll be wanting you to 'wrap it before I tap it'," said Annette.

The clerk only looked puzzled and quickly glanced outside the window. A clear, blue sky smiled back. There wasn't even a chance of rain, or snow. Sometimes she really hated this job.

"Here's your change, ma'am," said the clerk.

A little smile crept across Annette's face. "Uh-oh," I thought. "I know that smile." She leaned in and I could barely hear her whisper, "Are you a Freya? Because this Valkyrie would like to comfort you."

"No refunds or returns without a receipt," said the clerk.

Annette slowly winked at her, "We can keep it Loki if you want."

The clerk took a step back, "I really need to get back to shelving books now."

24

Annette gave a little laugh. Picked up her books and turned to me, "Come on, Kevin. Time to study."

"I was going to order *300* and give her my number. You know, so she can call me," I said.

"What are you thinking? She's much too young for you," smiled Annette.

Annette haughtily walked out the door. The door chime tinkled as the door slammed shut behind her. The black cat on the counter opened one eye, and went back to sleep.

I decided not to grow a beard, but I would take steps to prepare for the big heist. For Bill, that meant putting in a little extra gym time, and he invited me along.

The first day was back and delts, and that means dead-lifts. He was super-excited for the trip, and had even dug up his old CD with the soundtrack to *Conan the Barbarian*, the first one, not that B movie with Grace Slick.

Bill popped open the gym's community CD player, selected *Anvil of Crom*, and started loading an Olympic bar in the middle of the floor with 45 pound plates. He hunted around, needing to strip a couple of weights from the bar on the bench press.

"I wish people would put their weights away when they are finished. A neat gym is a safe gym," said Bill loftily.

"Don't you think I should start light? I haven't been to the gym for some time," I said.

"Muscle memory, Kevin. The body knows. Besides, what doesn't kill you, makes you stronger," said Bill.

"Nietzsche said that," I replied.

"Haven't heard of 'em. Come on, Kev. You'll be fine," said Bill.

"Nietzsche is dead," I replied.

"Should have used a spotter. You have me," said Bill.

"I'm sure my body is going to remind me of today, tomorrow," I replied.

I wandered off to the other side of the gym, looking for a couple smaller plates so I didn't get a hernia for Christmas. Bill continued to 'clean' up the weight room. He bent over to pick up a couple of hundred-pound dumbbells that someone had left by a bench.

"Someone must have been doing curls. Doesn't anyone put away anything in this gym? I'm not their mother," complained Bill.

As Bill was stripping 45-pound plates off the leg press, two gym rats entered. They were wearing matching weight-lifting belts. One was stroking his well-groomed goatee. They surveyed the scene to see who was there and almost tripped over Bill's heavily-loaded bar in the middle of the gym floor.

"What is that doing there?" said Mr. Goatee.

26

"Uggh, what's that horrible noise? Does someone think that's music?" replied the other gym rat as he pulled on a pair of spotless weightlifting gloves.

"How am I suppose to perform my curls to that?" said the first gym rat.

Bill came across the weight room with a big, rat-eating grin. He had two 2.5 pounders and a pair of clamps for the bar. He slid the weights on, put on the clamps, and chalked up his hands.

"Time to dip, grip, and let it rip," smiled Bill.

"You better not fart in here," I replied.

Bill bent down, got a good hand position on the bar, lifted up, and knocked out a good four or five repetitions. He let out a yell that would make his barbarian character proud. He gently put the bar down, smiled, and clapped his hands, resulting in a white cloud of chalk dust.

"Now that I'm warmed up, we can get to some real weight," said Bill.

The gym rats just stared at Bill from the squat rack as they prepared to do their curls.

Bill waved at them, "Hey guys, are you going to be using those 45's over there?"

I just shrugged my shoulders and prepared my body to lift with my legs and not my back...

I believe it was Sun Tzu in *The Art of War* who wrote, *"Victorious warriors win first and then go to war while defeated warriors go to war first and then seek to win."* The key to victory is preparation and one can't be properly prepared if one is dehydrated. For that there is beer, or wine, if you prefer.

In a D&D party, every character has his role to fill, and Tom's character is the procurer of supplies, both mundane and magical. It was only logical that it was Tom who chose to buy beer for our trip, but this is the real world, and it was decided that it was best for Barry and me to accompany him.

Tom doesn't do anything by half measures. He grabbed a shopping cart and started to make his way through the recently-remodeled "Beer Cave" at the local takeout pizza joint. The place sits on the outskirts of town, and usually is empty. I guess the owners figured putting in more beer would attract more people. It attracted us.

Tom had already put several six packs in the cart, and he was still browsing. "The adventure of a lifetime deserves a great beer," insisted Tom.

"Or several. I didn't even know that Pudgies had shopping carts," I said.

"Oh, they don't. I borrowed Barry's. Beer, beer, hard cider, what we really need is some mead. A proper Viking raiding party would take some mead along with them," said Tom.

I helped Tom search the shelves for mead. Tom was considering settling for a nice hard cider when a clerk strolled by. He was young with a bad case of acne and his name tag was on upside-down. He looked like he was perpetually confused.

Tom put on his best aristocratic airs, "Excuse me, good sir. Are you employed by this fine establishment? I am seeking nourishment in the form of elixir. I am in need of something to quench my thirst. I am seeking mead."

"We have Pabst Blue Ribbon on sale. Mead just doesn't sell that well around here. We usually only carry a few sixes for the tourists, and your friends just came in and bought everything we had left," answered the clerk.

"Nay, that could not possibly be the truth, young knave. I am the chosen one. The one ordained to procure the golden nectar. It is my quest!" proclaimed Tom.

"Dude, it had to be. They talked all pretty and were dressed up all fancy. Just like you," replied the clerk.

"Damn Rennies," said Tom disdainfully.

Tom gave the shopping cart a shove toward the checkout counter and rammed Barry as he turned the corner. It's like running into a castle wall. Barry dropped a huge armful of snacks unceremoniously into the cart.

"It looks like you are expecting a siege, Barry," I said.

"I got a little of everything. Something salty, something sweet, some protein for Berserker Bill," said Barry.

"Uh, do you think you got enough for the trip?" asked Tom sarcastically.

"Forget the mead. We needed to procure snacks for the trip," said Barry.

"You do realize it's only an hour trip to the museum?" asked Tom.

"I know, but with rationing, this should last until we get to the city," replied Barry.

"Didn't your doctor tell you to watch your blood pressure? All those salty snacks can't be good for you," I said.

"Blah, my doctor also told me to stop eating bacon cheeseburgers, and to go fishing to relax. I hate fishing and I love my bacon," said Barry.

"Fine, Kevin and I will grab more snacks if you go ask the clerk if they have any beer sippee cups. Annette threw mine out," said Tom.

"I'm going to need something to read on the trip. Kevin, do you have the latest copy of *Museum Replicas* at home? My brother-in-law has mine," said Barry.

"We have got to get you another hobby, Barry," said Tom and I together.

The problem with living alone is that I'll never find my kitchen table again. My table is always covered with junk mail, magazines, books, pens, and coupons for cat food that I never end up using. I eat on the ugly couch.

"It's time to draft a plan. Since you are a master of planning, and I'm the party leader, it appears we are elected," I said.

"Where am I supposed to find a place to layout the graph paper?" asked James.

"Just clear a spot. Put it on a chair, but not the one by the window; that's Loki's chair," I said.

"Now I know why we game at Annette's house," said James.

James looked at the mess and decided it was time to take a moment for inspiration. He placed his pen behind his ear and grabbed the copy of *Museum Replicas* that I was going to take for Barry to read. He paused at the image of *Glamdring*.

"Did Gandalf use *Glamdring*, or was that Thorin Oakenshield?" asked James.

"Thorin used *Orcrist*, the 'Goblin Cleaver', until he lost it in Mirkwood. Any first level knows that. Did someone place a modify memory spell on you?" I asked.

"How would I remember if they did? I'm just tired. I'm not sleeping well. My back's been bothering me," said James.

"Well, don't mention it to Bill. He'll blame your lack of musculature in your post-kinetic chain, and have you doing power cleans," I said.

"I need to focus. We can't just barge in there and steal the Viking longboat. We need to work harder on our plan," said James.

"The supreme art of war is to subdue the enemy without fighting," I said.

"More *Art of War* quotes? Really? That's not helpful," said James.

"It's a deep and meaningful quote," I said.

"Except the party always chooses to fight, even when I strongly hinted there was an alternate choice. Even that time when you were virtually surrounded, without your favorite magical weapons, naked, and in the dark," snorted James.

"I did suggest diplomacy," I said.

"You know the half-elf has infra-vision? You didn't think to look for another exit?" said James.

"We had Barbarian Bill," I countered.

"I've been thinking," James said. "We need an inside man."

"Or woman," I replied.

"What are you thinking?" asked James.

"Annette used to be a marine," I said.

James laughed and snapped his fingers, "And once a marine, always a marine."

"Exactly, I figure she can infiltrate the museum's defenses, and BAM, we're in!" I shouted.

James looked doubtful. "I don't know. It's not much of a plan. A museum has to have a pretty good security system. Some of those treasures can't be replaced. They're priceless."

Nevertheless, I was feeling pretty confident about my idea. "It's just like the other night in the campaign against the lich king. We had to infiltrate the tower to complete the quest. None of us thought we'd be able to do it."

James nodded his head, "Yes, security is only as strong as its weakest link."

"We get Annette to take care of the guard. We roll in with the gear to move the boat, and roll out," I said.

"You guys walked through the front gate of the castle by dressing Tom's thief as a court jester. That was brilliant, and funny," said James.

I chuckled, "It sure was. Only Tom would think of something like that. Worked like a charm."

"He got spelled with Otto's Irresistible Dance, flamed by a fire ball, struck twice by lightning, encased in ice, aaand he died," said James.

"Well, yeah, but it's not like there's going to be a lich waiting for us at the museum. Besides, the cleric resurrected Tom," I said.

James removed his laptop from the bag of holding he carries everywhere, and brought up the museum's website. He started to copy the floor plans onto graph paper.

"The party is going to have to deal with the lich once his withered corpse reforms. Discovering how to destroy the phylactery and where it's hidden, is going to be a quest in itself," said James.

"I can't wait to get back to it. Maybe on Christmas break? We'll all have more time then," I said.

"The party shouldn't rely so heavily on Barry bringing characters back from death's cold, dark embrace. He could have failed his roll," said James.

"We always come through in the end," I said confidently.

"Will the party be devoured by cacodemons? Only the DM knows," cackled James. "Anyway, the next adventure is all in a folder in my bag if something comes up," said James.

"We are not letting Barry run another campaign. So, speaking of campaigns, what do we call ours? If it's going to be official, we need a name. Then we'll be sure to go through with it," I said.

"I don't know if that always holds true. We never did implement *Operation Firefly in a Jar,*" said James.

"The name was too long, and Barry used all his vacation time that year to go fishing. It wasn't practical anyway. Fox is never going to bring back *Firefly*. It's wishful thinking, and where were we supposed to keep Nathan Fillion?" I asked.

"Yeah, that would have pretty much ended *Castle*. Hmm--we have ships, Vikings, how about we call it

34

Operation Sea Stead?" said James.

I smiled, "Annette would be proud that you were paying attention to her lecture, but how about something with more bite? I like *Operation Ragnarok*," I said.

"Twilight of the Gods? I love it!" said James.

"Come, let us sing the song of our people," I laughed dramatically.

Together James and I sang the beginning of Led Zeppelin's *Immigrant Song*. We might not have the words right, but we had spirit.

Ah, ah.

We come from Wellsboro land of guns and hoes,

Of the midnight beer runs where the alcohol flows.

We'll get hammered by god, and drive our longboat to new lands.

To murder the chords, and sing and cry.

Valhalla here we come.

Strategy without tactics is the slowest route to victory. Tactics without strategy is the noise before defeat.

OK, it's another quote from Sun Tzu. I never thought I'd be able to use all those quotes. A plan of action is just a plan until it is put into action. It was time to let the party in on the plan so we could get to the action.

James was sitting at his usual place at the head of the

table, but instead of character sheets and handfuls of dice, there were photos of the museum, maps, floor plans, and of course, Bill's petition for "Bring Your Claymore to Work Day."

James looked around the table and cleared his throat, "Are we ready to proceed with *Operation Ragnarok?*"

Bill jumped to his feet, excitedly. "Hell, yeah, I'm ready to rock!"

Annette just show her head and said, "No, Ragnarok. 'rahg-nuh-rok'. In Norse mythology, it's the final battle at the end of the world, in which gods and mortal men will be destroyed by monsters and darkness."

"Oh, you mean like *Gotterdammerung?*" said Bill.

"Exactly, like the opera by Wagner," agreed Annette.

Tom began to hum *The Flight of the Valkyries*.

"Right composer, Tom; wrong opera," smiled Annette.

"Opera? I was talking about the goth band from Holland. Man, they rock," said Bill.

Annette shook her head again, "Wagner's *Ring Cycle* was a major influence on Tolkien's *Lord of the Rings*."

"We're not after a ring," said Barry. "We're after a Viking longboat so I don't have to go fishing this summer. I don't even LIKE fish!"

"If we come back with a ring, we could put it through Bill's nose," said Tom.

"No, I had my ear pierced, but it got torn out when I was bouncing. Bouncers shouldn't wear any jewelry. Though

36

one of the bouncers likes to wear a skull ring in case he has to punch someone in the head," said Bill.

"We need to focus and go over the plan James and I crafted. First, we'll rent a moving van, like a U-Haul," I said.

"With cash! It's always with cash on TV. That way the cops can't trace it back to us. We should use a false identity, too. I could get us one of the fake IDs the bar confiscates," said Bill.

"Why waste the money? We'll just use my boat trailer. I can't wait to sell that damn boat of mine," said Barry.

"Isn't a boat with a dragon head, hauled behind a Hummer going to be just a little conspicuous?" said James.

"Well, we could throw a tarp over it, but yeah, good point," answered Barry.

Bill picked up the copy of *Museum Replicas* and immediately turned to the bookmarked page. It was the page showing the claymores, of course.

"I'm prepared for the adventure. I've already purchased the liquid refreshment," said Tom.

"I've been lifting extra hard, and I polish my claymore every day," said Bill.

"That just sounds so wrong," said Tom.

"I've been studying all aspects of Norse Mythology, as well as practical pick-up lines, drug interactions, and sentry elimination techniques," said Annette.

"Annette, this is supposed to be fun adventure. No one is going to get hurt. We are going to steal--I mean, pilfer--a boat. Let's not plan on killing anyone," said James.

"Oh, fine, I just don't want to get rusty," pouted Annette.

"We'll leave after work on Friday," I said.

I thought the school day would never end; I swore the second hand crawled. I felt like someone crammed me in a container and forget to punch holes in to let me breathe, and if I had one more person ask me for permission to go to the bathroom, I was going to go berserk.

Finally, three o'clock came and I rushed home to feed Loki, and to go over the floor plans one more time while waiting for the rest of the gang to show up. I started to think this wasn't a good idea. I'd never make tenure if I were caught. Who'd feed the cat if everyone I knew was staying at the blue roof inn?

Bill came hoofing up the driveway, pushing Barry's shopping cart full of beer and snacks. He pulled a beer out, popped it, and handed it to me.

"Where's everybody?" asked Bill.

"We're waiting on Barry. It seems like it's taking him a long time to rent a stupid truck," I answered.

"That means there's time to get some push-ups in," said Bill as he dropped to the icy sidewalk, and cranked out ten strict military style push-ups.

"So, where's your claymore that you can't stop talking about?" I asked.

"Damn, I knew I forgot something. I was focused on my core. I'll sprint home and get it," said Bill.

"Might as well wait, here comes the gang," I said.

Annette, Tom, and James arrived, emerging from Annette's minivan. I laugh every time I see it. I still can't believe that rough, tough Annette drives a minivan. I'm still not going to call her a soccer mom. I happen to like my nose how it is, unbroken.

Bill did one last explosive push-up and jumped to his feet as a dented U-Haul chugged into the driveway. "Shotgun!" shouted Bill.

"Fine, but I'm driving. The van is rented in my name and I want to get the full security deposit back," said Barry.

Tom looked disdainfully over at the van," We're not all going to fit in that cab."

I thought how this would be the perfect opportunity to get rid of the ugly couch. "We could throw my sleeper sofa in there, and then we can leave it at the museum. My ex left it here. I hate that damn couch. It's time for a changeling."

"Is that a good idea? There could be DNA evidence," said Bill.

"There's just crumbs and cat hair. I've already searched it for pocket change. The authorities could try to pin it on my cat, but he always has an alibi," I said.

"It's going to be too stuffy in the back and I need air. I am NOT riding in an enclosed space with a bunch of sweaty guys. I'm riding up front," said Annette.

Annette never talks about her time in the marines. She's still Annette, but she has a quicker trigger, and sometimes she gets this look in her eyes, and I find myself imagining how much war she's seen, but then I shrug it off. I mean the woman does teach eleventh grade geography and political science.

"Something isn't sitting well from lunch, and I'm feeling kind of nauseous. Do you mind if I take the window seat?" said James.

"It's cool with me. This is a sleeper and there will be lots of room. I swore the next time I moved this ugly beast would be the last. I hate this couch. Help me get it out of my house," I said.

Bill and Barry helped me carry the sofa out the door one last time. It really was the last thing my ex-wife had in the house, except the curtains. I hate those curtains, too. It was good to see the couch leave. The fold-away bed had to flop out and pinch my fingers one last time before we managed to shove it into the van. Leave it to my ex to get one last hit in.

"I told you it was a beast to move, but now I have an excuse to buy a new couch," I said.

Tom, Bill, and I all climbed into the back of the van. Barry pulled down the back door and secured it. As the van pulled out of the driveway, my nosy neighbors might have

40

heard the muffled voice of Bill shouting, "I need to get my claymore!"

The trip was relatively uneventful. Bill kept asking Barry to turn back so he could get his claymore, but Barry refused. Barry threatened to duct tape Bill's mouth after he started singing *100 Potions of healing on the wall*, but I had only brought one roll of duct tape, and that was reserved for the plan.

Annette couldn't stop shivering. James had the window down in case he had to toss his iron rations. I didn't know if he was sick or nervous. I've seen James eat things that would make a dog puke, and I've never taken James for the nervous type. I realized he must actually be sick. He did look a little green around the gills, or maybe yellow. I told myself to talk to him later about cutting back on the beta-carotene.

Thankfully, the museum is only an hour drive. Luckily, it only took us an hour and a half, as Barry worried incessantly about getting the full security deposit back, and drove fifteen miles under the speed limit, and made full, complete stops at every stop sign.

Once we finally got to the museum, Barry pulled the van slowly into the parking lot. He parked far away from the other vehicles.

"I don't want to get a scratch on it. Want to be sure to get the full deposit back," said Barry.

I didn't have the heart to tell Barry that no one ever gets the full security deposit back, but I was just glad to finally be able to stretch my legs and hand out the designated assignments. I know the worst scenario in a horror movie is to split up, but this was a simple heist. It's not like we were going to run into a dragon.

"We're going to split up and get familiar with the layout of the museum," I said.

"Scooby Dooby Doo," yelped Tom.

"It always looks a little different in person, and the Viking display is a limited time exhibit. This is going to be our last chance to do what we came to do before it sails back to Denmark," said James.

"I'll take my little brother. I'm used to babysitting him," said Annette.

"I'll do my best to keep Bill out of trouble and out of the Peter Paul Rubens section. You know how he likes big, beautiful woman, but we're on a mission," said Barry.

"Hey, Rubens was a well-rounded artist," quipped Tom.

"Beauty is in the eyes of the Beholder. Get it? Beholder, like in the *Monster Manual*?" said Bill.

"Yes, Bill! We get it!" moaned everyone.

"I'll see if I can keep Barry out of the snack shop. We're supposed to explore, not snack. I do happen to appreciate the Renaissance artists. I especially enjoy the depictions of Madonna and child, and yes, I appreciate a woman with curves," said Bill.

"Hmmmm, Reubens...I sure could go for a nice Reuben right now," said Barry.

"Is Madonna pregnant? Or is she adopting again? It's a shame she's adopting all those foreign babies and putting American babies out of work," said Tom.

"Do NOT, tell that joke at church, and that's Angelina Jolie...I think?" said Annette.

"We'll grab supper after we do some recon. We have to do this now before the museum closes. James, you're with me. You have your orders and notebooks. Take some notes so we can compare," I said.

In retrospect, I'm glad I insisted on notes. They came in handy. I never expected I'd be using them to write a memoir. I always expected my first book to be a space opera. I guess you write the book you have to write.

"Let's get this done," I said before everyone entered the museum.

It'd been a long time since I'd taken time to visit the Rockwell Museum. I appreciate art, and it's only a short drive to Corning, but life has a way of getting in the way. I have papers to grade, dragons to slay, and of course, beer to drink.

I never really understood Picasso's Blue Period, or why Van Gogh sliced his ear off, but I suspect a woman had something to do with it. They usually do, and that's why I like Western Art. Give me a grand, rugged landscape any day, uncomplicated and open.

James and I decided to explore the Western Art section. James had his pen out and was taking copious notes. I was checking out a classic Remington painting that was surely inspired by the untamed wilderness that will always define the American spirit, just like the firearms company that helped tame the American West.

"Now, this is what I call art, James. None of that Post-Impressionism for me, I like my art realistic," I said.

"You enjoy Frank Frazetta's art, and those depictions of women aren't realistic," said James.

"You've seen *Death Dealer's* battle-ax? I've been married. Believe me. It's accurate," I said.

"I'll take your oath on that, but I want to be sure to spend some time in the Viking Exhibit. It's crucial," said James.

"Sure, that's what we're here for, but we have lots of time before it's night at the museum," I said.

"Not all of us have all the time in the world," muttered James.

"Look! They have *End of the Trail*, cast by James Earle Fraser. It's one of my favorites. I have an old T-shirt with that on it, or I think so. My ex probably used it as a cleaning rag," I said.

44

"Uggh, I've always found it depressing. It symbolizes the effects of Western expansion. The brave is shamed and defeated. The American Indian has reached the end of his trail of tears, pushed into the cold waters of the Pacific. It always made me sad," said James.

"Hmm, I never saw it that way. I see a warrior, worn from battle, but far from defeated. I always saw it as a symbol of resilience and strength. He's just taking a breather before getting back into the fight," I said.

"I'm running out of fight, Kev," sighed James.

"What do you mean? We're just getting started on this little operation," I said.

"I'm all in for *Operation Ragnarok*. I'm just afraid it's going to be my last adventure with you guys," said James.

"Last adventure? You aren't getting married, are you? Even Barry's wife lets him play D&D. Gets him out of the house," I said.

"No, I'm never getting married," said James.

"Good choice! Me either, not again anyway. You aren't afraid of getting caught? I'm not planning on getting caught either. Have to make tenure," I said.

"We aren't going to get caught. We have a plan, and we have Annette; that's not what I mean," said James.

"You aren't thinking of giving up D&D and going to *Pathfinder*? That'd break Barry's heart. We could take a break and play *Call of Cthulhu*, or maybe even try a board game if you need a break from being Dungeon Master," I said.

"That's not what I mean. You know I'd never leave the group, but I've been sick," said James.

"It's the Christmas season. There's always some bug going around. You'll feel better. It's not like you're dying," I said.

"Actually, I am dying," said James.

"Sure, sure we're all dying. I'm a day closer to death than I was yesterday. If you want to play *Vampire: The Masquerade* just say so, but remember Bill will insist on being a werewolf instead," I said.

"I'm not joking. I have cancer," said James.

I was stunned. "Those tests aren't always conclusive, are they? Did you get a second opinion? Are you sure?" I asked.

"Yeah, I'm sure. I waited too long to get it checked out. It really wouldn't have mattered. Pancreatic cancer has a way of sneaking up on you.

"You can get treatment though, right?" I asked.

"The latest tests show there's not much they can do. Treatment really isn't viable. I have a few months, tops, and I can be 'comfortable' which probably means doped out of my mind," said James.

"When were you going to tell us?" I asked.

"I didn't know how to bring it up, and it's Christmas. I didn't want to tell people I was dying at Christmas. I'd appreciate it if you didn't tell the others. I don't want to take away from the excitement of tonight's adventure," said James.

"Well...Okay, if you really think that's for the best. Come on! Let's see us a genuine Viking longboat, complete with dragon head," I said, trying to sound cheerful, but feeling my guts turn to lead.

Meanwhile, Barry and Bill were strolling through the other wing of the museum. Barry, the ever-dutiful accountant, was taking copious notes. Bill, on the other hand, was enjoying himself immensely, looking at paintings and sculpture, and reading plaques.

"Pay attention, Bill. We're going to have to get the equipment through here later tonight, and everything will need to fit. I'm glad James was able to borrow those walker stackers from work. How'd he get permission for that?" said Barry.

"Getting that answer is only going to give you more questions. Don't worry. I'm a pro with one. It's easier to operate than a forklift. You just walk behind them, and let the electric motor do all the work. I'll just go right up the middle. They don't take up that much room."

"It's not a football game, Bill," said Barry.

"Relax, Barry. I have it covered. Live a little. Soak up some culture while we're here," said Bill.

"I'm a sponge. I soak up lots of culture, thank-you-very-much. We need to pull this off without any gremlins getting in the way, or I'm going to have to go fishing next year, and the year after that," said Barry.

"Why do you hate fishing so much?" asked Bill.

"It's boring. You sit in a boat all day and drown worms and get sunburned, and my socks get wet. I hate wet socks. AND my wife insists that I take my brother-in-law," said Barry.

"If you hate it so much, why did you start?" asked Bill.

"I thought it'd be a good way to spend some time alone and think, but my brother-in-law never shuts up. Besides, I hate fish. Give me a nice steak so rare a good vet could still save it, and a beer so cold it makes the bones in my fingers tingle," said Barry.

"You should take up weightlifting. It prevents osteoporosis and it's very peaceful. It's like moving meditation that helps you build muscle," mused Bill.

"I've seen you lift and there's nothing peaceful about it," said Barry.

A huge sandstone arch loomed ahead of Bill and Barry. The face of the stone was covered with hieroglyphics: the beginning of the Egyptian Exhibit.

"Oh, the Egyptian Exhibit. You know the Egyptians worshiped cats?" asked Bill.

48

"Yes, Bill every fifth grader knows that," replied Barry. "But did you know that some of those kitties received the same mummification techniques after death as the humans?" asked Bill.

"No, Bill, I can't say that I knew that. Is the bar holding a trivia night on Thursdays again? Let's find that snack shop, and then meet up with the others," said Barry.

"Can you imagine a movie like that? *Abbott and Costello Meet the Kitty Mummy...*" said Bill. Bill held out his hands straight in front of him, starting to shamble like a mummy making kitten sounds. "Mew, mew, mew."

"Bill, that's annoying as hell. Knock it off," Barry complained. Then, to soften his criticism a little, he added information to Bill's game of Egyptian trivial pursuit. "I do remember reading about Anubis, Egyptian God of the Underworld. He was an embalmer. He was responsible for removing a person's heart when they died. He would place it on a scale, and weigh it against the deeds of their life. If their hearts were heavy with evil deeds, he would devour them," said Barry.

"Now you're making me hungry, Barry. I'll buy you a Reuben," said Bill. "Let's go!"

Meanwhile, Annette and Tom were standing with several people in front of a sword display, doing their best to blend in with the crowds. An attractive female museum guide asked the group if there were any questions.

Tom approached the woman and smoothed out his shirt. "Yes, let me 'axe' you a question. Is that a sword, or are you just happy to see me?" asked Tom.

Annette rolled her eyes and poked her brother in the ribs. The guide looked slightly perturbed, but answered Tom's question smoothly.

"That is an ulfberht, a well-crafted sword of the Viking Age that utilized steel of higher purity and carbon than most of its peers in the region," said the guide.

"Hey, that's a coincidence. I named my sword too. I bet you can handle a sword pretty well. How'd you like to swing mine?" said Tom with a wink.

Now the museum guide looked disdainfully at Tom.

"Thanks, but I'm more into the sheath than the sword," said the guide.

"Put away that short sword of yours, Tom. I love hearing about Ulfberht from an experienced guide. So many people go on and on about Japanese swords. They think the katana are the greatest swords ever forged, but give me a good, solidly-crafted broadsword any day," said Annette.

Tom just rolled his eyes and started to wander off to see the display of Viking helms.

"Hey, where are the horns," questioned Tom's voice from a distance.

The guide was a petite brunette with startling green eyes. Annette and the guide exchanged appreciative glances.

"Exactly, you don't need to fold good steel, and showing a sword that starts as molten steel is pure Hollywood fiction; that's Bronze Age technique. Any good bladesmith knows if a sword is to have any strength to it, it has to start as a good chunk of steel," said the guide.

"Uggh, and no quenching in blood. And why men insist on calling a fuller groove a 'blood groove' is beyond me. Anyone who's wielded a blade knows it's to make the sword lighter and easier to swing. I much prefer to be fast and first with my point. Swords weren't made to go edge to edge. That's just going to get you a broken sword," said Annette.

"At least you could make a wakizashi out of it!" yelled Tom from down the hall.

"Can't I have one intelligent conversation without your interrupting?" yelled back Annette.

The pretty guide ignored the sibling argument, and went on enthusiastically, "Exactly! Sword fighting was more often a brawl than a Hollywood action movie," said the guide.

The rest of the crowd had dissipated. It was only Annette and the guide who remained, talking in front of the display.

"My name is Cassandra, but you can call me Cassie. I get off at nine o'clock. What say we get a drink? There's a nice little bar down the street called the *Honky Tonk*," the guide smiled.

"My name is Annette, and I'd love to get to know you better. I'll be there."

The *Honky Tonk* was a small, Western-themed bar with the expected country music playing in the background. Annette sat alone at the bar nursing a drink. The rest of the gang was across the room, sitting at a darkened corner table.

James reached into his pocket and pulled out a handful of gaming dice, saying, "You're in a tavern..."

"I check for traps," said Tom.

I just shook my head. You can take the gamers out of the game, but you can't take the game out of the gamers. I whispered to James and Tom, "You're in a country bar with Lady Antebellum playing in the background and patrons wearing cowboy hats. Try to blend."

Bill looked around. "I knew I should have brought my claymore," he said.

"You're in a bar, not a tavern," I said.

"It's NOT *Highlander*," said Barry.

"That means there can be MORE than one!" said Bill excitedly.

"Shhh, quiet, who's that guy walking towards Annette?"
I said.

Annette quietly sat at the bar drinking her scotch,
neat. A rangy man in faded blue jeans and a denim shirt
approached her.

"What's a pretty little gal like you doing all alone in a
place like this," asked the wanna-be cowboy.

"It should be rather obvious. I'm partaking of liquid
refreshment while I await my evening companion," said
Annette.

"How about I buy you a drink, pretty lady?" asked the
cowboy.

"As you can plainly see, I already have one," answered
Annette.

"How 'bout me and you doing a little two-step?" asked
the cowboy.

"How about you let me finish my drink in peace?" said
Annette.

The tall, lanky cowboy looked perplexed. Just as it
seemed like he was going to ask Annette another question,
the attractive guide from the museum came slithering into
the bar.

Her hair was down now and she had on make-up--scarlet
red lipstick, mascara, eyeliner, plus heels and a tight dress.
She glided up to Annette and took a sip of her scotch.

"Strong and undiluted, just the way I take it," said
Cassie.

"Of course, di-hydrogen monoxide kills, you know," said Annette.

Cassie gave her a little, knowing smile. "It's a major component of acid rain," she said.

"And it's used in industrial solvents and coolants," said Annette.

"It really should be banned. We should start an online petition," answered Cassie.

The good old boy was looking dazed and confused, but he wasn't one to give up easily, "Why, here's another pretty little filly. Don't you worry none. I'm a long drink of water, and I'm here to wet your whistle. There's plenty of me to go around," said the cowboy.

"There's plenty of room for you at the other end of the bar, too," replied Annette.

Cassie looked amused at the cowboy's awkward attempt to get anywhere with Annette, but wanted to diffuse the situation. Just at that moment, *Girl Crush* by *Little Big Town* started playing.

I got a girl crush...

With that, Cassie grabbed Annette's hand and led her onto the dance floor. The cowboy shook his head, then tipped his hat and moseyed off.

"So, I'm guessing you aren't the strong but silent type?" asked Cassie.

"Talking softly and carrying a big stick only works if you are Teddy Roosevelt," said Annette.

54

Annette and Cassie slow-danced. Meanwhile, the guys sat at the table looking rather out of place. All except for Barry who sipped a beer and looked like he was rather enjoying himself.

"Now I know why we start all our D&D adventures in a tavern. This sure beats fishing with my brother-in-law," said Barry.

"Tom, you never told me about your sister," said Bill.

"What, that she prefers women? Why would you need to know that? What business is it of yours?" answered Tom angrily.

"Calm down, dude. I knew that already. You never told me she could dance like that, and with a prosthetic leg. I'd never know if I didn't know. She sure is graceful. I have two right feet when it comes to dancing. Get it? Right feet?" said Bill.

"Yeah, we get it, Bill. You're a leftie. We know that, because you keep telling us that," said Barry.

"There was an entire clan of Scots that trained left-handed. There's even a spiral staircase in their castle with a reverse spiral. A left-handed swordsman has the advantage of surprise against a right-handed opponent," said Bill.

"Great, you better not have two right hands if you actually have to swing that damn claymore of yours, Bill. So, just what's the plan, James," asked Barry.

"I don't have my claymore, because you wouldn't go back for it," said Bill.

"A simple plan is best. Annette gets her drunk, goes back to her place, gets her security badge, changes into her clothes, and we mosey right into the museum, or rather Annette does, and then she opens the doors for us," said James.

"Hey, that plan sounds awfully familiar. There's not a lich around here, is there?" asked Tom.

"We won't be encountering magic or the supernatural in this scenario," replied James.

Annette and Cassie were moving to the rhythm and dancing closer. Annette's hands began exploring Cassie's body.

"I think Annette is already trying to get into that dress," said Bill.

"We don't need her in that dress. Her tour guide outfit, you dumb orc," said James.

The song came to an end, and Annette and Cassie slid off the dance floor walking toward the guys.

"They're coming this way. Everyone act natural," I said.

Tom took a die from his pocket and rolled.

"I rolled a natural 20! There's no way they'll notice us," said Tom excitedly.

"That's not natural," said James.

"No, really; it's a natural," said Tom.

Everyone just shook his head and expressed wonder at Tom's exceptional luck, except Bill, who was looking off into the distance. He took a deep drink of his beer, and muttered under his breath, "I wish I had brought my claymore."

Time passes fast in a bar, even in a country bar where you don't exactly blend in. I think beer might have something to do with that. We partook of several frothy pitchers as Annette worked the details of the plan.

Annette and Cassie prepared to leave the bar after taking obvious pleasure in each other's company, and enjoying several more drinks and dances. It was good to see Annette look happy. They made a beautiful couple, and by the glances I observed, I wasn't the only one who noticed.

Cassie wove a little as the couple made their way to the exit. Annette was giggling and smiling, but I've known her a long time. She wasn't as intoxicated as she played it. Cassie, however, was tottering like a drunken Snow White.

The couple exited the bar and entered the chilly December night. Cassie wrapped her arms around her body, shivering.

"I could warm you up," offered Annette.

"My apartment is just up the street. You could come up for a night cat. I mean a night cap," said Cassie.

"Would you like me to tuck you in and tell your little kitty a goodnight story?" asked Annette.

"Hmmm, maybe. What's the story about?" asked Cassie coyly.

"Shhh, did you hear that?" whispered Annette.

Annette and Cassie stopped to listen. They had just passed an alley. A stifled scream broke the silence. Annette quietly reached down and smoothly drew a small silver knife from her boot before entering the alley.

"Where are you going," whispered Cassie.

Annette's senses were alert. The hair on her arms stood up. Her eyes weren't adjusted to the dark of the alley, but her ears caught the scuffle of feet, the tear of fabric, and a low growl of a rough voice.

"If you'd stop strugglin', this would go much easier for you," said the gruff, male voice.

Annette heard a muffled sound, followed by the rough voice calling out, "You shouldn't have gone and bit me, bitch."

Annette could just barely see a hulking, dark shadow looming. Then, a shaft of moonlight shone into the alley, illuminating a brute of a man. Annette lunged out with her knife. A grunt of surprise and a curse bounced off the walls of the alley.

"I was going to ask you nicely to take your hands off the lady, but I'm a little short on patience this evening," said Annette.

"I don't know who you think you are, but you've made a hell of a mistake," said the deep voice.

58

"Yeah, I shouldn't have worn boots with such a high heel, but I'll still kick your ass," said Annette.

"You are dead!" cursed the thug.

"You gonna talk me to death, or are we going to dance? I'll lead," said Annette.

The brute was confident fighting a woman, but he hadn't met Annette in a bad mood. He darted forward and lashed out with a hay-maker right that Annette easily saw coming. She ducked, slashed the knife across his ribs, and bobbed up behind the thug.

The thug yelped out from the gash and turned his ugly head back and forth searching the shadows for Annette. He couldn't see her anywhere, but spotted the beautiful Cassie illuminated in the entrance of the alley, and started lumbering towards her.

"Well, there you are," said the thug.

Annette grabbed a trashcan lid and brandished it like a shield, in her left hand. She leapt forward and attacked the man from behind by shield-bashing him with the lid in the back of the head.

The man stumbled into the brick wall of the alley. He shook his head and looked back only to have another 'shield' smashed into his face. He slid down the wall and slumped to the ground. Annette delivered a fierce kick to his head, just to be sure.

"Here's one for getting my knife dirty," spit out Annette.

Annette glanced around the alley, but it appeared to be empty. The victim had made a run for it. Annette threw down the trash can lid on the man, bent down to wipe her knife on the man's shirt, and sheathed the knife in her boot again.

"Just what is your story?" asked Cassie.

"Oh, I teach high school. Now, how about that night cap?" asked Annette.

Annette was a smooth operator. She knew the score. We wanted to rush right out of the bar and follow as soon as she left, but we knew to give time for Annette to work her magic. Once James finished his beer, he announced, "that's enough of a head start. Let's go!"

James was the first out into the street. He looked left and right.

"Damn, which way did they go?" asked James.

"I'll track them," said Bill confidently.

"Bill, you don't actually know how to track, do you? Sure, you track when we are role-playing, but there's no roll for this. Besides, this is a city covered in asphalt and cement," said Barry.

"Just call me Lord Baltimore; that's right, I can track anybody, over anything, day or night," replied Bill.

"Hey, you got that from the movie, *Butch Cassidy and the Sundance Kid*," I said.

"I know. It's an American classic. It's one of my favorites," said Bill.

"It's a Western. I didn't know you liked Westerns," I said.

"Of course! Westerns symbolize humanity's struggle against nature. They embody masculinity, and everything a man should aspire to be...honorable, reliable, and self-sacrificing. With a society organized around codes of honor, justice, and vengeance. It's just like *Conan*, but with saloons and six guns," lectured Bill.

I looked oddly at him.

"And Joss Whedon's *Firefly* is basically an outer-space Western: it's obvious that the Browncoats were inspired by the Johnny Rebs of the American Civil War," said Bill.

Only then did I remember that Whedon had once given an interview where he credited *Killer Angels* written by Michael Shaara. All these years later, and I'm still angry at Fox for canceling it after not even a full season, idiots.

I grew sadly pensive and nodded my head in agreement with Bill. The whole gang concurred.

"I miss *Firefly*," said everyone in unison.

"I think Annette and her new friend went that way," said Tom, pointing up the street.

"And how the hell did you come to that conclusion? You suddenly learn to track, too?" asked Barry.

"No, but I know my sister, and there's a guy over there taking a dirt nap," said Tom.

Tom was pointing to the entrance of an alley. A large man was lying prone, half-in and half-out of the alley. I couldn't see his face; there was a trash can lid covering his head.

"It always was my sister's job to take out the trash at home," said Tom.

We ran over to check on the man. Tom bent over to pick up the garbage can lid. The man groaned and rolled over.

"You gotta help me. Call the ambulance...and the cops. I was mugged," moaned the man.

"Was the mugger about 5 foot ten?" asked Barry.

"Yes, at least, maybe taller," moaned the man.

"Did they attack you with a little, silver knife?" I asked the man.

"Uh, I think so. Everything happened so fast. There was a knife and it looked silver in the moonlight, but it was huge," groaned the man.

"Did they walk with a bit of a limp, the right leg?" I asked sarcastically.

"Yes, yes! Oh, you know the fiend I'm talking about. Thank god. They must be on the ten most wanted list. I'm lucky to even be alive," shouted the man.

"Was it a woman?" asked James.

"Oh, it was," the man sobbed, "She must be on steroids, or PCP, or those bath salts or something."

Barry kicked the man in the head, knocking him unconscious once again.

"See, I told you Annette came this way," said Tom as he dropped the garbage can lid on the man's face, and walked away.

Annette and Cassie climbed wooden stairs to a second floor apartment. Annette leaned into Cassie for a lingering kiss. As their lips parted, Cassie reached into her purse to retrieve her keys. She fumbled around, pulled them out, and demonstrated how much she had drunk by dropping her keys.

Annette bent over to retrieve the keys before they fell off the landing. Cassie bent over at the same time and they bumped heads. Rather than turning this close encounter into another opportunity for a kiss, Cassie just fell over and stayed sitting by the door rubbing her head.

"I thought you were hitting on me," slurred Cassie.

"If you wanted to bump uglies there's an easier way to let me know," said Annette.

Annette picked up the keys and after several attempts, found the right key for the right hole.

"Not so hard. I just had to imagine there was a little hair around it," said Annette with a little wink.

"You just want to take advantage of me. Besides, I just had a Brazilian and opted for the 'Hollywood Wax'," slurred Cassie.

"I really do, but there are some things I need to discover for myself. Now, let's get you inside and into bed. Then, I can start the expedition," said Annette.

Annette swung the door open, and helped Cassie to her feet. Together, they stumbled through a small living room and into the bedroom where Cassie flopped onto the bed, and immediately passed out.

Annette looked longingly at Cassie spread out on top of the bed covers. Cassie made her bed every morning? Annette turned down the bed, rolled Cassie over, tucked a pillow under her, and turned her head to the side. You know, just in case she vomited.

Annette covered her up, and gave her forehead a tender kiss. Then she started sorting her closet in hopes of finding a museum uniform.

"Come on, c'mon. It has to be in here somewhere," mumbled Annette.

Annette riffled through several neatly hung items, including a French maid outfit, a tavern wench outfit, a Sailor Moon cos-play, a Star Trek uniform, and even a Princess Leia slave outfit.

"This is killing me. I knew she was my type," moaned Annette.

Annette was getting frustrated. The only luck she was having was bad. She turned back to visualize how Cassie would look in a gold bikini, and then looked down. There was the museum uniform, thrown carelessly on the floor.

Annette went over to collect the clothes and spotted Cassie's magnetic badge on the nightstand.

"Score! It looks like I will just walk through the back door or at least the employee entrance" smiled Annette.

Annette began to take off her clothes exposing the cold plastic of her prosthetic leg, and changed into Cassie's clothes. The skirt was a little short, as Annette is quite a bit taller, and the shirt was tight since Annette is well...full-figured is one way to put it. Tom would say stacked if she wasn't his sister.

"It's passable. I'm pretty sure the guard isn't going to tell me no," said Annette.

She adjusted everything, applied her makeup, put her own clothes in a bag, pulled out a pair of high heels, and got ready to walk out of the apartment.

"Now to find the guys and proceed with Operation Ragnarok," said Annette as she walked into the night.

The guard shack sat beside a closed gate. Annette strutted up to the shack with a sway in her hips, dressed as a museum guide. Her top button was unbuttoned and her hair had that just-got-out-of-bed look.

It was after midnight and the old guard had his nose buried in a book--*Outlander* by Diane Gabaldon.

"Yoo hoo, oh, guard," Annette called out, sweetly.

The guard was so startled that he dropped his book.

"Can I help you, miss?" asked the guard.

"Yes, you can. It seems I left my book on antique swords and daggers in my locker," said Annette.

"Sorry, miss. Employees are only supposed to use the east side entrance. This side is just for truck deliveries and other services," said the guard.

"I can't. My identification card wouldn't work. My cat chewed on it, and now the display just gives me an error message," pouted Annette.

The guard looked bored. He yawned and stretched his arms, and came outside the guard house to look at the identification card.

"I recently inherited this silver dagger. It was my grandfather's prized possession and I wanted to identify it correctly," said Annette.

Annette drew the little silver knife from her stocking. The guard began to look interested.

"That there looks like a sgian-dubh. It's a Scottish knife often worn with traditional costume. It's sometimes called a last resort knife," said the guard.

Annette softly purred, "I just love a man who knows his blades. My great, great-grandfather was a Scot."

The guard puffed up his chest and said, "I do pay attention when I make my rounds, but I'll have you know

I'm part Scot on my mother's side. I have a dress kilt, and even signed the online petition for 'Bring your Claymore to Work Day.' Tradition is important to me," said the guard.

Annette shyly held the dagger out. "Would you like a closer look? I'm just a guide and I don't know much about daggers and swords," said Annette.

"Oh, the sgian-dubh isn't a dagger. It's a single-edged knife. Daggers almost always have two cutting edges. Although some Persian daggers are single-edged, and the stiletto has no cutting edge at all," said the guard to Annette.

"All thrust?" said Annette innocently.

Annette approached the guard with the knife. She held her hand straight out.

"Here, take a look at this and let me know what you think," said Annette.

"Careful there. A knife isn't that different from a firearm, in that you should never point it at anyone unless you plan to stick them with it," said the guard.

Annette moves with a grace that no one with a prosthetic leg should be able to manage, especially in high heels. She quickly closed on the guard and held the knife to the underside of his chin.

"Please keep your hands to your sides. You are correct. It really is a knife of the last resort," said Annette.

Annette whistled and Tom, Bill, James and I appeared.

I carried the only duct tape I could find, a roll of Justin Bieber-themed duct tape, and Tom brought out a rag from his back pocket.

"Sorry about this. It's the only duct tape I could find. It's my niece's, and she's really into crafts and Canada," I said.

I started wrapping the surprised guard with the duct tape, nice and snug. Tom approached the guard with the rag.

"Tell me, does this rag smell like chloroform to you?" asked Tom.

"Using all your best pick-up lines tonight are you, Tom?" asked Annette.

The guard's head slumped forward and I gently lowered him to the ground.

"You better gag him in case he wakes up and makes like a shrieker before we get out, and don't forget to switch off the security cameras," said James.

Tom found the control for the gate, and opened it. This was the signal for Barry to pull the van up and through the gate.

"We're in. Close the gate so the situation looks normal. You better prop the guard up with his book, so that gag isn't so noticeable," said Barry.

Tom helped me get the guard back into his chair, and situated. I bent over to pick up the dropped book.

"*Outlander*? I loved that movie. Space dragons and Vikings in the same film? What's not to like?" I said.

"No, you silly Owlbear; that's Diana Gabaldon's fantasy romance of two time-crossed lovers. You should read it some time. It's awesome," said Annette.

I opened the book to the first page and started to read.

"Uh, Kevin, maybe you can pick it up at the bookstore at home...later. We have a Viking longboat to liberate," said James.

Night at the museum: we had successfully infiltrated the main gate, and not even one fireball. I never thought we'd actually go through with it, or get this far. No problems, and events were going smoothly. All we had to do was get to the Viking display, and grab the ship.

Bill opened the door to the docking bay, and wheeled out an electric loader with a box of bungee cords and ropes. "This looks way spookier than when we were in here this afternoon," said Bill.

"The Viking display is this way. We just need to seize the long boat, get it loaded, and get the Hades out of here," said Annette.

"Where's the bathroom?" asked James.

Barry grabbed a mace from the wall, and made a few practice swings.

"I never did make it to all the exhibits I wanted to see when we were here earlier," said Barry.

"How about we come back next year...You know, if we aren't in jail? Let's get done what we came here to do. Morning isn't that far away, and I'll never make tenure if I'm caught," said Annette.

"You doing OK, James?" I asked anxiously.

James was not looking well at all. He was pale and drawn. Night time is usually James time, but he was looking tired. Now that I knew, I could see it. The circles under his eyes, the weight loss. I wanted to say something, but I wanted James to be the one who told the others.

"I'm alright, but not sure how much help I'm going to be pulling at the oars," replied James.

"That's why we have Bill and Barry along. We don't call Barry the Bear for nothing," I said.

Tom spoke up, "I always thought it was because..."

"No, Tom. Just no," I interrupted. "Let's get this party started."

I loved the carving of the dragon's head on this longboat. It was particularly fierce, and the craftsmen had taken the time to put a large jewel where the eye should be. I don't think it was real, but the effect was definitely cool.

Bill was just finishing putting the last electric dolly under the keel, and tossed a loop of rope over to me to help secure the load.

"All we have to do is haul this baby back to the dock, get it loaded, and get out of here," I said.

"Everyone grab some rope and pull. Breakfast is on me," said Barry.

"Can you guys go ahead without me? I have to find a bathroom," said James.

"We'll get this towed back to the loading dock, but hurry. We don't have all night, and Barry won't offer to buy breakfast again this decade," I said.

We started the slow trip back to the dock. It wasn't hard once we got the ship onto the loaders. We couldn't go fast, but Bill wasn't kidding when he said he was good with one. I caught on pretty fast.

James wandered through the Viking exhibit looking for a good place to spew his guts. He had filled the prescription for some pain killers, but they made him pretty nauseous.

James paused before one of the many displays to rest and read.

The tools displayed at this exhibit were excavated from a bog in the Lapania area, one of Europe's largest bogs. The anaerobic environment and presence of tannic acids within bogs can result in the remarkable preservation of organic material.

This bog has produced several well-preserved bog bodies, fully intact, in addition to several tools and weapons including this short-handled hammer. The hammer was made to resemble Thor's hammer, the mighty Mjolnir.

"I wish it really was Thor's hammer. Casting lightning would be awesome, but Mjolnir was said to wield powers of healing as well as destruction. Feeling like I didn't have to hurl every ten minutes would be great," whispered James.

Just saying that, James began to feel nauseous once more and looked for some place to vomit. He took a cover off a trash can and puked inside.

"Any port in a storm," said James as he wiped his mouth.

James looked longingly at the hammer. "Why not? I'll never get another chance like this," he mumbled.

James crawled under the rope barricade and made his way past the other artifacts. He gently touched the head of the hammer, and let his hands slide down the shaft.

"I'm glad Tom isn't here to see this. I don't want to hear another phallus joke today," said James.

"Whosoever holds this hammer, if he, or she, be worthy, shall possess the power of Thor," whispered James as he went to pick up the hammer.

With a slight grimace of pain, James removed the hammer from the display. It was heavier than he thought it would be. Bolts of lightning surged from the head of the hammer, and through the Viking exhibit. A large clap of thunder followed.

"Oh, crap! I didn't know it was loaded!" yelped James.

We were just finishing loading the longboat. We had to leave the ugly sleeper sofa on the loading dock, but I had planned on that all along. Have I mentioned that I hated that damn couch?

Tom was busy filling up the surrounding space in the van with whatever he could find...spears, maces, shields, and a plastic Viking helmet, complete with horns, courtesy of the museum gift shop.

"What in the Hel was that noise?" asked Barry.

"Someone brought the boom," said Bill.

"Has anyone seen James?" I asked.

"Tom, hurry up and finish your Christmas shopping. Everyone else, let's go look for James," said Annette.

Something stirred in the shadows. There was movement in the Viking exhibit. James glanced around. Several of the well-preserved bodies were starting to move.

James got a tight grip on the hammer, and started to run. He didn't get far. We were coming to look for him. He stopped running and tried to catch his breath.

"James, why are you breathing so hard?" asked Annette.

James slowed down, took a deep breath, and said, "Roll for initiative. It's..."

A nearly unbearable stench of death and decay followed James. It seeped into my nostrils, and made Barry gag. It made me wish I hadn't eaten that extra serving of hot wings at the bar. I couldn't stop from gagging.

"What is that awful stench?" gagged Annette.

"It's the smell of death. Sorry, sorry, it appears I've woken the dead!" yelled James.

"You mean zombies! It's the damn Zombie Apocalypse and I don't have my double- barreled shotgun, or my claymore? I told you I should have brought my claymore," pouted Bill.

"It's not zombies; it's worse. It's draugr!" yelled James.

"What the hell is a draugr?" asked Bill.

"Undead creatures from Norse mythology. Superhuman strength, control of weather, able to change shape and size. You know, as seen in the video game 'Skyrim?'" said Annette.

"Oh, Viking zombies, cool," said Bill.

"Interesting, it doesn't appear they are mythological, but quite real," said Annette.

"Uh, not cool, not interesting! They're real! The dead walk!" shouted Barry.

"I suggest we arm ourselves and prepare for combat," said Annette calmly.

Annette turned around, and saw that she needn't have bothered stating the obvious. We'd prepared for this our entire lives. Barry hadn't even put down the mace he had picked up minutes ago. He truly was a cleric at heart.

Annette grabbed a shield off the wall. I snatched a nice long sword. Tom came running down the hall wearing his plastic helmet complete with horns and brandishing a katana he had stolen from some exhibit.

"Next time, you can bring your fucking claymore, Bill! Now how about shutting up and using that huge battle ax?" I shouted.

"Battle ax? Cool!" shouted Bill.

With that, the battle began. These were not your typical *Night of the Living Dead* zombies. The draugr were armed with swords and shields. They didn't move like zombies, but rather more like slightly arthritic athletes. It didn't look good.

"They sure don't move like zombies!" yelled Barry.

"Well, at least it's not *28 Days Later*, or *World War Z* zoms!" yelled James.

"Uggh, *World War Z*, a whole lot of CGI and Brad Pitt staring into the camera," said Tom.

Tom sliced at the neck of the draugr in front of him, lopping its head off with the katana.

"I learned that one from watching the *Walking Dead*. Now there's some quality zombie television," said Tom, sidestepping a draugr who approached on his left.

Barry smashed the head of an un-dead with his mace. "I think the zombie genre is overdone. They need to come up with something else," said Barry.

Annette smashed the closest draugr with her shield. Barry continued to smite away at the wall of shambling death, and Bill the Berserker was earning his name. He might not have had his preferred claymore, but he was damn good with that two-handed battle ax.

"I sure wish I had a helmet," said Bill.

"Just keep your clothes on this time, Berserker Bill," laughed Annette, beheading a corpse without missing a stroke.

James was awkwardly wielding the hammer he had picked up in the Viking exhibit. It had such a short handle. I didn't think it was the best weapon choice for James.

He definitely wasn't doing well. The draugr in front of him looked bigger than all the rest. Hell, it was bigger!

"Is it just me, or are these damn things getting bigger?" I yelled.

"I told you they can change size and shape. I also read that they can control the weather, too," yelled Annette.

"Great, maybe it'll get cloudy with a chance of meatballs," quipped Tom.

A bolt of lightning surged past Tom, and hit the wall behind him.

"I thought you promised there wouldn't be a lich?" yelled Tom.

"Hey, it could have been a cloudkill spell!" yelled Barry.

The dragur in front of me lashed out with his sword and shattered mine. Yeah, I know. You aren't supposed to fight edge-to-edge with swords, but playing with bamboo shinai does not prepare you for an eight-foot corpse taking a swing at you.

I raised my shield and took my beating until Barry could come to my rescue and decimate its head. Barry really is a brute.

"It'd be useful, actually, to have a cleric in the party right now," I said.

Barry started to sing in his deep, bass voice, *If I Had a Hammer.*

If I had a hammer
I'd hammer in the morning
I'd hammer in the evening
All over this land...

"Hand me another sword, Barry," I said.

James was getting backed into a corner. The hammer was looking too heavy to wield, and he looked exhausted. He was looking like he was about to get his head split in two. So, I introduced that bearded zombie to some cold steel, and chopped its head off.

"Thanks, man. Heads up!" shouted James.

I was starting to enjoy myself. There's nothing like staring death in the face to make you feel alive. "No, James, heads off!" I laughed.

I never did see the draugr behind me. It's the ones that you don't see that get you. Next thing I know, I'm looking down and seeing two feet of steel where my beer belly begins. That's the last thing I remember...

The first thing I remember is waking up on the cold, hard ground. It appeared to be dusk, and it was freezing. Colder than it had been, even though it was early December, and there was snow. We hadn't had any significant snowfall yet this season in the Twin Tiers.

Up ahead, I could just make out a huge tree thrusting towards the sky. Among the thick boughs was a light. I decided it was time to get off the frozen ground.

"Did anyone get the license plate of the frost giant that ran me over," I asked the sky, because it looked like I was the only one here.

I squinted into the distance and saw a huge hall made of timbers. I sniffed the air and took in the smell of roasting meat. It made me hungry.

"What is that delightful smell? It reminds me of my uncle's BBQ," I said.

I gave a shrug and followed the path that seemed to lead towards the gigantic tree and the hall. As I approached, I saw a huge door open to the cold. The light was so lively and strong, the hall couldn't contain it.

The warmth poured out in waves, and felt good against

my skin. It was so inviting that I don't think I could have stopped myself from entering if I wanted to.

Tables filled the hall and men filled the tables, all manner of men. There sat a dark-skinned man all dressed in buckskins. He stabbed a haunch of meat with a giant fork. To his left sat a man dressed in plate armor, minus the helmet, his beard dripping wine. He raised a tankard and made a toast to a man sitting across from him. I couldn't make out the words. The rather small man was dressed in khakis and had smudges of dirt and blood on his face.

The tables were lined with meat and beer, and all of it served by scantily-clad, attractive women. One grabbed me by the arm, and led me to a seat in front of a huge T-bone steak and a rather large mug of beer.

I was hungry. My mouth watered. I smacked my lips. They were dry. There was nothing in the world I wanted more than an ice, cold beer. I raised the mug to my lips, and that was the last thing I remembered...

I woke up feeling hung-over and tired. James was at my side asking me if I was doing OK. The hammer was in his right hand and glowing an electric blue.

"I could use a Gatorade and an espresso, and I think I have a hole in me," I said.

I looked down to see my shirt had a huge hole in it. The shirt was ruined. It was my favorite Star Wars shirt, too, but I felt OK. Not great, but I didn't see a gaping wound, and that's always a good thing.

James appeared much more vital. There was a healthy glow about him. I don't know how to describe it. He looked strong. He stood up and gave a yell worthy of a hero, and swung that hammer like a warrior born.

The skull of what looked like the last standing draugr was smashed into pieces by James. He raised his hammer and yelled again in triumph. It looked like the battle was over. It was time to get out of here and to grab a hot shower.

But we had missed something, just like we had not thought to look for the lich's hidden soul. I guess we were distracted by the corpses, and my being dead. It can really mess with your perception. All during the battle, a menace had been growing. The shadows coalesced to form the outline of a giant wolf. It was huge. It was frightening. It was fucking real.

The monstrous wolf sprang from the shadows, and landed among the party, sending shock waves through the museum and knocking everyone to the ground. Damn it. I had just made it to my feet, too.

The giant wolf growled and let loose with a heart-stopping howl that caused the entire building to shake and caused a nearby wall to collapse. In a flash, the beast was

80

gone, leaping through the newly-made exit.

"What the hell was that?" I said.

"If I had to guess, I'd say that was Fenrir," said Annette.

"If I had to guess, I'd say that was a bad thing?" said Barry.

"In Norse mythology, Fenrir is the wolf that devours the world," answered Annette.

"Yup, that's a bad thing," said James.

We looked around in open-jawed wonder. The entire museum was a freaking, chaotic, evil mess. Pieces of dried-out corpses clung to the ceiling--what remained of it. Broken weapons and skulls covered the floor, and the shattered remains of displays were strewn down the entire length of the hall.

We were standing there in stunned disbelief. We didn't know what to do next. A cold breeze blew in through the gaping hole that Fenrir had used to exit the building.

Bill picked up a brick and tossed it through. A mummified cat, complete with burial wrappings, chased after it, "mew, mew, mew."

Bill started to hum *Walk like an Egyptian*...

"Should we tidy up before we leave?" asked Tom.

"Yeah, we don't want anyone to know that we just unleashed Ragnarok," said Annette sarcastically.

I could only stare at the rubble at my feet. I couldn't move. I couldn't think. I didn't know what to do. It wasn't fear. It wasn't anything. If you stare into the abyss, it stares back, and its eyes are red.

Annette grabbed me by the arm and pulled, "Come on. We have to get out of here! The morning shift will be here soon" yelled Annette.

"We can't leave that creature roaming the countryside," said James.

"We could call animal control?" said Barry.

"I just knew I shouldn't have left home without my claymore!" said Bill.

Dawn had broken cold and clear. Barry slammed down the overhead door of the U-Haul. He didn't seem quite so worried about getting his deposit back. Tom jumped into the driver's side, and we all crammed into the cab.

"Please return your trays to the upright position, and fasten your seat belts!" yelled Tom.

Tom turned the keys in the ignition and revved the engine. He pushed the gas pedal to the floor. Grinding gears and biting his lip, he approached the gate at the highest speed that clunker of a van could muster. Tom never even slowed down; the gate never knew what hit it.

"Lady and gentlemen, in case of an emergency, oxygen masks will drop down in front of you, and you will hear me scream like a little girl!" screamed Tom.

"You really should slow down. You're going to attract attention!" yelled Barry. "Damn it, Tom, I'm not going to get my full deposit back now!"

"Perhaps you haven't noticed, but there's a giant, earth-devouring wolf on the loose, and the museum is... uh, broken. How do you suggest that we NOT attract attention?" yelled Annette.

"I don't know. Tom could try driving casual!" Barry yelled back.

I remember a lot of yelling at this point. My head was starting to clear, and I was starting to feel a little better. Not much, mind you, because I was starting to remember that we had apparently unleashed the end of the world. It was a lot to take in.

"So, which direction would a world-devouring wolf head?" asked James.

"Norse by Norse west?" shouted Tom from the driver's seat.

I spoke up, "We could try following the path of destruction."

I pointed out the window to the torn-up road, the flattened cars, and the uprooted trees. "I don't know where he's headed, but I'm pretty sure he went that way."

Tom turned on the right turn signal and pulled out. I remember the radio in the van started to play *Highway to Hell* by AC-DC. I really could have used something to drink.

The van crept along the city streets. Tom was driving slower than I've ever seen him drive. It's not because he wanted to. He had to. There wasn't much of the road left. I had no idea what we were going to do next.

"Fenrir has got to be starving after a thousand-year fast. I think he'd go where he could get his fill of sheep," said James.

"Wal-Mart! He's heading for Wal-Mart!" shouted Tom.

"I've seen *The People of Wal-Mart*. I'm not so sure we should stop him," said Barry.

"I'm not sure that we can stop him," said Annette.

"Onward! No straw death for me! We've stared death in the face and we are still alive! Do you want to live forever?" exclaimed James passionately. He seemed really excited, or maybe he had just re-watched *Conan the Barbarian*--the original, not the re-boot with Aquaman.

"Well, actually, yes, I do. It's a marvelous age we live in, and I'd like to see more of it. Besides, I'm not really that far from early retirement, and I still have all my limbs. Oh, sorry about that, Annette. I forgot," said Barry.

"Well, if it were the Zombie Apocalypse happening, I'd head to Sam's Club. There's everything there for your End of Days needs, and you have to be a member to get in," said Bill.

The entire van filled with groans.

My head was clear: suddenly, I knew the answer. "Well, I've watched both the *Dawn of the Dead*, and the re-make. So, I think we should drive towards the..."

"Mall!" shouted the rest of the van.

"Cool, maybe they'll have a claymore store," said Bill.

Meanwhile, at the mall, Santa was preparing for another endless day of sticky fingers, grumpy parents, and countless demands. The fat man in red turned to Santa's little helper.

"It's time for me to drag my red velvet-covered ass out there and start my shift. You coming?" said Santa.

"Cheer up, old man. It'll be over soon. Just a few more weeks until Christmas and then we're both done," chuckled the elf.

"Ho, Ho, Oh, I just want this holiday season to be over. My back aches. My feet are swollen. My cheeks have gone numb from smiling. I don't think I'll ever smile again, and we've only just started," said Santa.

"Let's take it one brat at a time. Just get through today, and I'll buy the first round at the Honky Tonk tonight," said the elf.

"Does this red suit make my ass look fat? I feel bloated," said Santa.

"Are you gluten sensitive? You should cut back on your refined carbohydrates. The Paleo Diet is really working for me," said the elf.

"Let's invite that cute elf in wrapping and see if she wants to get naughty. It'd save me a trip Christmas Eve," laughed Santa.

The little helper sighed and looked over at the gathering crowd. It was going to be another long day. He took a deep breath and prepared himself emotionally to deal with the complaints of parents, and the whining of children.

"The children, they just keep coming and coming," sighed the elf.

"Let's get this circus started," said Santa.

"Once more into the breach," muttered the elf.

"I wanted to be a rock star and I have to face that this is as close as I'll ever come to screaming, adoring fans," sighed the fat man in red.

The screams were coming closer and getting louder. There seemed to be some sort of commotion in the mall, but it hadn't reached Father Christmas's throne. "Hmmm, well, it is the holiday season. Damn, I sure hope it's not because of that filming session. I needed the money, and being an elf doesn't pay as well as it should. Well, it is the Christmas season, and anything can happen," thought the elf.

The crowds were getting more restless. Parents began to push each other in line. Something was wrong. The elf could feel it. One child started screaming, then another, and another...

The manager of Victoria's Secret looked up from a rack of red and white lacy bras. Was that a scream coming from central court? 'I hate the Christmas season.' She sadly shook her head and thought of the nice bottle of red wine waiting for her at home.

People dropped their bags and brightly-wrapped packages and began to run. Santa and the elf could hear the snarl and growls above the roar of the crowd, except it no longer sounded like a crowd at all. It sounded like a pack of wild dogs, or one pissed off, enormous wolf.

Fenrir was filled with joy--so much prey, so much movement. He dashed through the herd slashing to his right. He knocked over kiosks and displays. He lashed out to his left. He bit the head off a large deer with a bulbous nose. No blood slaked his thirst. He growled in frustration.

A cute female elf dived into the Frosty the Snowman display to avoid the sharp, gnashing teeth, but Fenrir sprung after her. A moment later his monstrous head popped out with a jolly little elf hat stuck between his teeth, and blood on his jowls.

A hipster with tiny Christmas bulbs in his beard pulled a smart phone from his pocket. "I'm going viral with this." Fenrir's ears turned like a radar antenna. "I've never seen such huge carnassials. It's like I'm a member of the wolf unit on Game of Thrones. Damn, where the Wi-Fi. Why is my phone picking up nothing but static. What is that awful smell? WHYYYYY---"

Santa could only stare at the huge beast. He was a city boy: the only animals he'd seen this big were in the zoo, behind enclosures, where he was safe. He didn't feel safe now. Here there was so much screaming. There was so much blood. Santa wasn't safe. The elf bolted.

Fenrir turned his head and watched the elf scurry away. He turned his attention back to the not-so-jolly Santa Claus and stared at the man dressed in red wearing a big, white beard. The creature was familiar. He opened his mouth and seemed to grin.

"Odiiiiiin..." growled Fenrir.

The U-Haul chugged into the parking lot of the nearest shopping mall. It had to be the right place. I could feel it. It was Saturday. At least I thought it was Saturday. I think it was Saturday. It had been late Friday when we started out, but I'd been in a different time zone, and place, and time, or maybe it's a dimension? I was back from the dead, and I hadn't even started my Christmas shopping.

The parking lot was pretty full for early in the morning. There wasn't any sign of the gigantic wolf Fenrir, but it's a big mall. The party was looking low on hit points. We'd been up all night. We've been in a battle with the evil undead. The Age of Man appeared to be coming to a close, and it would soon be the Twilight of the Gods. It'd been a long-ass campaign.

"What are we going to do now? We can't just stroll into the mall with swords, shields, and a mystical hammer," I said.

"If your only tool is a hammer, then everything is going to look like a nail," said Tom.

"I don't see why not? We'll just say that we're with the Society for the Creative Anachronism, and that we are here for an exhibition," said James.

"We aren't in garb, and Kevin has a Star Wars shirt with a bloody hole in the middle," said Barry.

"I was in the SCA once," said Bill. "I thought it meant the Society for Chaos and Anarchy."

"No, you fought a knight of the realm who was dressed in full plate armor, and you only had carpet armor on. It was a demonstration by the local shire of the SCA on the Green. Their weapon master chided you for not being chivalrous. He mentioned something about black flag tournaments and told you to not come back," said James.

"He moved so slow with all that heavy armor and huge shield. Too bad I can't go back: It was a great workout, and much cheaper than therapy," said Bill.

"You kept turning your opponent to the sun and wouldn't stop when he shouted for quarter," said Barry.

"Hey, I didn't know the guy. Why should I give him any money?" asked Bill.

Everyone groaned at Bill who just shrugged his shoulders.

"They didn't even let me use my claymore. Something about it not being period. Hell, no, it's more like an exclamation point," said Bill.

"Well, the knights of yore are all dead. I guess it's all fun and games until gunpowder, matches, and cluster bombs are invented," said Annette.

"Speaking of cluster fucks, just how are we supposed to kill a wolf the size of a bull moose?" asked Barry.

"We don't need a cluster bomb. We have Mjolnir," said James.

"You can nail him with the hammer," said Tom.

"It's just a hammer," said Barry.

"It brought Kevin back to life," said James.

"Awww, he must have just been knocked out," said Barry.

"He had two feet of steel sticking out of his guts," said James.

"I'm pretty sure I was dead, but I did get better," I said in my best British accent. It's not that great an accent. I'm not sure if Barry actually got the Monty Python reference.

"Fine, you have a magic fucking hammer. I have a piece of metal from the Bronze Age and a replica wooden shield," said Barry.

90

"Actually, it's from the Viking Age, which ran approximately from 793 to 1066," said Annette.

"Whatever," said Barry.

"It's a very nice shield, Barry," said Bill.

"Thank you," said Barry.

"You could even say it's boss," said Tom.

"I have a plan. You guys distract the wolf, and I'll smash him over the head with the hammer," said James.

"Well, I see why you always get to be the Dungeon Master. That's a brilliant fucking strategy," said Barry.

"Oh? And what would the 'Party' do? You'd all just yell 'attack!' and charge the wolf," said James.

"How do you stop a charging wolf?...Anyone? You take away his credit card," said Tom.

"No, I'm a cleric. I'd say a blessing first," said Barry.

"I don't use a shield because a claymore is a two-handed weapon," said Bill.

"I think we should go with what we know," said Annette.

"True, now isn't really the time to change tactics," I said.

"ATTACK!!!" shouted the hardy, but foolish band of adventurers...

We prepared to enter the mall.

"Oh, an Olive Garden! Can we eat there when we get done?" asked Bill.

"Focus, Bill! Forget about the endless breadsticks for a minute!" I said.

As we entered the mall, we were greeted by flickering lights and shouts in the distance. It's a big mall and we didn't know which way we should go, but the hammer seemed to pull James to the right.

As we walked down the wide, dark hall, a dwarf dressed as an elf ran past us screaming. "I told you we were at the right place," I said.

"Is that Santa's helper?" asked Bill.

"Santa's a little short on help right now, I think," said Tom.

"Mjolnir seems to be guiding me," said James.

"Again with the magic hammer," said Barry.

"You can accept a humongous, mythical wolf, but not the mystical hammer keeping the proverbial genie in the bottle?" asked Annette.

"Hey, I didn't get through the entire museum. Maybe they had a petting zoo?" said Barry.

"With dire wolves?" said Annette.

"The situation is pretty dire," said Tom.

"A petting zoo? Now we have to go back. Maybe they have those fainting goats? I love those," said Bill.

A long, menacing howl echoed through the mall. We glanced at each other and continued on. What else were we going to do? The lights appeared to be off in most of the mall, but the atrium had a glass roof, and the morning sunshine sparkled through.

The central courtyard was a mess. Dead bodies were everywhere, as well as half-wrapped packages, and merchandise from various stores scattered across the floor. It was depressing, but at least no sleazy salesmen tried to sell us anything from one of the kiosks.

A pair of escalators rose up to meet a second floor that appeared to be the food court. James held the hammer aloft, and it pointed to the escalators, which weren't moving.

"Things are looking up," whispered James.

"Why are you whispering?" whispered Tom.

"So we can get initiative," whispered James.

We approached the steps and started climbing. Upstairs was indeed a series of fast food places with a central eating area. Many of the tables were knocked over, and the chairs scattered. The place was a mess, but there wasn't any moose-sized wolf.

"No wolf. Let's go check out Sam's Club," said Barry.

"It's obvious Fenrir has been through here," I said.

"Could have been a sale on tacos," said Barry.

"There in the back. It's like a cave," Annette pointed.

Tucked back in the corner was an arcade. It was dark with an occasional flash of color and sound.

"That's where I would hide if I were a wolf," said James.

We spread out. I don't know the proper formation to

attack a world-devouring wolf, but spreading out seemed like a good idea. I guess he'd have to kill us one at a time that way. It might not stop him, but maybe he'd get tired.

We approached the old arcade. The letters above the entrance spelled 'Time Out'. The sign kept flickering. First the 'Time' would light up, then go out. Then the 'Out' would come on, and then shut off. It was creepy.

"Looks like someone is out of time," said Tom.

Entering the arcade, we encountered only silence. It was too quiet. A low growl started to build to a crescendo. Fenrir bounded out from behind a row of video game cabinets, knocking Barry and Tom across the floor and out into the food court.

James lashed out with the hammer, but only connected with the screen of an old Pac-Man game. Shards of glass and plastic flew everywhere.

Fenrir snarled and turned to bite Annette, but she moved too fast. No longer where she had been, she thrust out with her lucky, last-resort dagger, sticking it in Fenrir's right eye.

The Great Wolf yelped and spun away from Annette, knocking into Tom who had just gotten back up from the floor and back in the fight. Bill swung with his great ax, but the result was not so great. He only managed to slice off Fenrir's tail.

Fenrir opened his cavernous maw to attack Tom anew. I was able to step in front and fend off the attack with my shield, which soon turned into a shower of splinters. Tom owed me a beer.

Barry had gotten to his feet, and managed to pound his mace into Fenrir's flank. I'd never seen Tom so pissed. He lashed out and pommeled Fenrir's head with the butt of his sword.

Fenrir shook his head as if to clear it. James decided to swing for a home run with the hammer. He barely missed, and the hammer passed by the snarling visage of the wolf. The wolf clamped down on James' arm, and began shaking his head back and forth like a terrier would shake a rat.

Barry smashed his mace against the flank of the giant wolf, but it seemed to have no effect. The wolf would not let go of James' arm. Tom stabbed the wolf with his sword, but still Fenrir would not let go of his prize.

James screamed and with a raw, wet tear, his right arm was torn off. James fell hard to the floor, and the magic hammer went skidding across the floor.

The wolf opened his mouth and grinned, "Tyrrrr," growled Fenrir.

I wanted to shut my eyes, but couldn't. I could see the broken nub of bone emerging from James' shoulder. It looked like a joint of ham. I couldn't do anything but stare. The damned demonic wolf trotted towards me. I no longer had a shield, so I dived behind some upturned tables.

Bill went ballistic. He lofted his great ax over his head, pulled his arms back, and gave the mightiest of throws. The ax flew straight at Fenrir and sliced off his left ear. Yeah, he wasn't doing so well with that ax. I wish he had brought his claymore.

"You'd be toast, mutt, if I had my trusty claymore!" roared Bill.

The wolf spun around and lunged at Bill. I guess he was pretty attached to that ear, after all. Bill managed to pick up a table just in time to take the brunt of the blow, but it left him pinned to the floor with only a cheap table between him and a mouthful of razors.

Annette sprinted to pick up the hammer. She was without a weapon, and her favorite dagger was sticking out of Fenrir's eye socket. She couldn't budge the hammer.

"Damn, this thing is heavy," swore Annette.

I ran over to help Annette with the hammer, as Fenrir was attempting to eat Bill's face. I was almost there, when suddenly Annette was not only picking up the hammer, she was making a mighty swing towards Fenir's blind side. The head of the hammer glowed a soft, electric blue.

Mjolnir made contact with the dagger of last resort, driving it farther into the eye. As the hammer made contact with Fenrir's head, blue-electric sparks flew, and ice crystals began to form. A sheet of ice spread out from the eye to the head, and down the body.

Fenrir's entire body quickly became encased in ice. The hammer wouldn't move. It appeared frozen in time. Annette couldn't let go. Then, the block of ice crumbled, spreading ice everywhere. Fenrir was gone.

Mjolnir shattered and a shock wave knocked everyone to the ground. Annette threw her hands over her face, but was blown backwards into an Orange Julius stand. I wondered if she was dead. I wondered if any of us would make it. I passed out.

I was the first to regain consciousness, thinking about how much time I'd spent baffled lately. I crawled over to James. He wasn't breathing. Blood was everywhere. I couldn't do anything. The other party members groggily made it to their feet.

Annette came over to help, but there was no helping James. He was beyond help. He was dead, and there was no magic hammer that was going to help bring him back.

"We have to get out of here, Kevin. The cops will be here soon," said Annette.

"We can't just leave him," I said.

Bill came over and gently picked up James. I could see tears in his eyes. I couldn't believe that James was gone.

"We leave no man behind," said Annette softly.

Tom went over and collected James' arm. "Leave no trace. We don't want to leave anything behind," he said.

Barry bent down to retrieve his battered mace. "Yeah, it's almost like it never happened," said Barry bitterly.

The letters above the arcade fell off in a shower of sparks.

The day was drawing to a close, with the sun setting. The U-Haul backed up to the boat dock at Ives Run, and we lowered the Viking longboat into the water. We placed James' body in the boat with a sword and shield across his chest.

"James deserves a funeral fit for a Viking chieftain," I said.

"No straw death for our favorite Dungeon Master," said Annette.

"You truly are in a better place," said Tom.

Barry and Bill prepared to shove the boat out onto the lake. Barry wiped a tear from his eye, and Bill sniffled.

"I'm going to miss you, buddy," said Barry.

"I should have brought my claymore, so I could give it to you," said Bill.

The boat launched and gently glided into the cold, silent lake in the growing darkness. Annette pulled out a bow, knocked an arrow, and Tom pulled out a lighter. He lit the arrow.

Annette drew and shot the arrow into the boat, setting it ablaze. We watched our beloved Dungeon Master burn as the ship burned around him. The jewel in the dragon's eye gleamed in the fire.

It was time to take the U-Haul back. I doubted Barry was going to get his full deposit back, but it didn't seem to matter. He still drove like a blue-haired grandma. Bill held his ax out the window in a final salute.

The van came to a complete stop at the stop sign before the entrance to the highway. Barry turned on the left turn signal, and the truck pulled out. It was time to go home.

We were home, but it didn't feel the same. It was time to get back to everyday life. It wasn't easy. It's tough not yelling at the idiot that cuts you off in traffic knowing that the only reason he's able to gab on his cell phone and exist is because of your sacrifice.

Annette went back to school. She earning her master's degree, made tenure, and adding Physics to her teaching repertoire. I'm proud of her. I knew she could do it. She said it's not hard, at least not after slaying Fenrir and helping to stop the end of the world. It did, however, morph her teaching style.

"OK, class, you have twelve +3 arrows in your quiver. If each arrow does 1 die 6 of damage, and you win initiative, will you be able to stop Ragnarok before Fenrir eats your face?" said Annette as she stands in front of her class with her hands on her hips, "Please show all your work."

Annette's also dating Cassie now. I'm happy for them. They make a nice couple, and we'll need another gamer if we ever have the heart to play again. Hey, we'll have two females in our party!

It just wouldn't be the same without James. I guess we could finally try something a little different. Maybe a board game?

I've had my eye on one based on the Cthulhu Mythos created by H.P. Lovecraft. It'd be a nice change to run from the monsters we encountered instead of challenging them to combat. We saved the world from Ragnarok. How hard can it be to save it from a squid-headed, elder god?

Bill is Bill. He seems unfazed. Oh, he misses James. We all do, but he's young, and he's Bill, after all.

He got new tattoos and he'll show them to you, even if you'd rather not see them. *'Bjorn to be Wyld'* on his right shoulder, and *'Life is Wyrd'* on his left. That's Bill for you.

Barry seems much happier and lighter in spirit. He started taking better care of himself and eating better. He even started working out again, and he finally sold the fishing boat. He hates fishing, so he told his wife that her brother can find another fishing partner.

Tom? He's still the smart ass. It'd take more than the end of the world to make Tom serious. He's still preaching to the choir, literally. He does a great fire-and-brimstone sermon, though the jokes do take a little of the edge off.

You should catch his early Sunday service some time, not that I make it to church often. It's hard to get up Sunday mornings when I have trouble sleeping Saturday night. Besides, I already know I'm going to a better place. I know what's waiting for me.

I finally listened to Bill and got myself a big, old claymore that I keep in my bedroom. I keep it nice and sharp. Every night before I go to sleep, I pull that big bastard of a blade off the wall and visit the land of Nod with it across my chest. I'm not going to make the mistake of being without a claymore.

Every night I think of James and I can just imagine him in my mind's eye, sitting at a table with a big smile, a huge mug of beer, a medium-rare steak, and a buxom blond on his lap. There will be no straw bed death for me.

You better save me a cold one, James...

Acknowledgments

I didn't write this book alone. Sure, I decided to come back to the store and write when I could have been reading, sleeping, or watching *Game of Thrones*. I was the one that turned an interesting idea into a useless screenplay that sat in a drawer.

It was my choice to turn that screenplay into a novella that I re-read and re-wrote until I hated it. I guess I did write it by myself, but I didn't create it alone.

My thanks to Tom Conte, who loved the idea and encouraged me to pound out that first outline: Tom even contributed several lines of dialogue for the character, Tom. My amazement to people like Bill Waltz and Becky Coolidge who love almost everything I write, even if I currently loathe it.

Love to my wife, Kasey Coolidge, who helped edit my many editorial mistakes. My appreciation to those who donated to the Kickstarter, so I could get my novella out to the masses, and my gratitude to Gary Gygax, the creator of Dungeons & Dragons, the man who helped fuel the imagination of generations.

About the Rockwell Museum

The Rockwell Museum is a real museum located in the heart of Corning, NY. The Rockwell is more than a museum! Displaying exquisite pieces, the Rockwell is a unique community center where people enjoy, connect, and reflect on the essence of the American spirit, character, and values through the eyes of American artists.

You won't see a genuine Viking longboat, but the museum does contain an extensive Western art section, including contemporary Native American art. The Rockwell Museum is the first and only Smithsonian Affiliate in Upstate New York, and they are guaranteed to be draugr free. Check it out for yourself at rockwellmuseum.org, but if you visit, please leave your claymore home.

About the Cover Artist

Always an artist, Annette Redman was drawing before she could speak. She loved art, but grew up hearing that artists starved. So she put her brushes away and pursued a practical career that did not include pencils and paints. She became a United States Marine, but some passions can't be contained.

One night while on duty, Annette was caught sketching. Instead of being punished, Annette was granted the opportunity to serve the Corps as a Combat Illustrator and achieved great things both as a Marine and an artist.

The Corps opened many doors for Annette and she continues her career in art. She devotes much of her time to teaching and encouraging people to pursue their passion. So many artists hide...Annette encourages all artists to believe in themselves and follow their heart. The only bad art is the art you bottle up inside—free yourself and create.

If you would like to purchase an original work of art, or commission an original work, please visit her website.

www.myartshack.wix.com/redmanart

About the Author

Kevin resides in Wellsboro, Pennsylvania. When he's not writing, you can find him at From My Shelf Books & Gifts, an independent bookstore he runs with his lovely wife, several helpful employees, and two friendly cats, Huck & Finn.

He's a Viking at heart, and when he's not sharpening his broadsword or mending his hauberk, he's writing more stories about intrepid gamers. Be sure to catch the next adventure, *Codename Cthulhu.*

You can write him at:

From My Shelf Books & Gifts
7 East Ave., Suite 101
Wellsboro, PA 16901

www.wellsborobookstore.com

Other Books by Kevin Coolidge

Kevin is also the creator of *The Totally Ninja Raccoons,* a children series specifically geared towards reluctant readers.

It's your classic trio with a twist. Think the "Three Investigators" meet the "Teenage Ninja Mutant Turtles" with a little "Ghost Busters" in the mix.

What started as an idea to score free food soon ends up giving the raccoons a glimpse into another world, a world of shadows, mysteries, and plots.

There are more things in heaven and earth than the raccoons ever dreamed. Cats are trying to take over the world. Monsters are real, and Chinese food really will make you hungry soon after you eat it. It's up to *The Totally Ninja Raccoon*s to stop it.

The Totally Ninja Raccoons Meet Bigfoot

The Totally Ninja Raccoons Meet the Weird & Wacky Werewolf

The Totally Ninja Raccoons and the Secret of the Canyon

The Totally Ninja Raccoons Meet the Thunderbird

Available at From My Shelf Books & Gifts, on the Internet at **www.wellsborobookstore.com**, your favorite bookstore, or wherever books are sold.

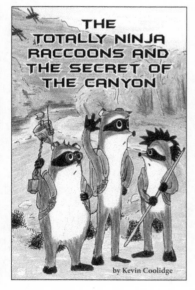

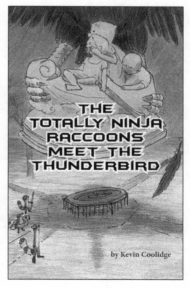

CPSIA information can be obtained
at www.ICGtesting.com
Printed in the USA
LVHW091354250719
625327LV00001B/48/P